Ordering Information:
Quantity sales. Special discounts are available on quantity
purchases by corporations, associations, and others. For
details, contact the publisher at the e-mail address above.

ISBN: 9781686363276
Imprint: Independently published

• • •
2

LIGHT MINUTES

ANGEL MANUEL TORRES, JR.

PROLOGUE

As in usual prologues, there is a time and place to infuse the characters and their own cognitive function to the plot. I have chosen a different route here, one that allows me to take the scenic route or the road less traveled. I would like to impart to you, the reader, a message worth following—a message about keeping one's heart open to different perspectives, whether it may be in the matter of light or dark. Moreover, to portray the illumination of a soul that is pouring over their community; perceptively aligning the positive delta with a combustion of outspoken words, in which I hope one would gain motivation from reading.

Time and space—the intangible dichotomy. Imagine a quadratic plain; there is an origin at the cusp of each ninety-degree angle. For each one-hundred-eighty degree angle, there are positives and negatives with slopes of space and time. One may call it the fourth dimension, but I call it reality. The reality of one's life happening, and everything that may happen—positive or negative, is inevitable. Timing is perfect, and our environment is where we are meant to be.

It is exhilarating being able to see different perspectives which can then be understood by their origin. The opposites attract each other. Neither time nor space is positive or negative. The cosmos are within our reach, and only time will tell how far one's reach can or will be. The cosmos can be interpreted in many different aspects. Astronomical thoughts to one's calling or destiny is the metaphorical reach to the Moon, Planet Mars, and beyond. As timing coincides with cosmology, it also correlates with will—what will happen, is bound to happen. Now that's an interesting topic, isn't it? What will happen will only manifest if our free will is sought out to take initiative for what should happen ... right? The planetary orbits are the parallelogram to one's reachable goals and aspirations. The alignment must be at its closest point for the best outreach possible.

At the core of this book, the energy has outpoured through the windows of opportunity to view different perspectives which can succumb into variations of height and width. I challenge you, as the reader, to figuratively take flight like a Bald Eagle or Neil Armstrong and his crew, and when reaching higher, I'll be sure to guarantee you of a wider horizon. One's viewpoint is the physical hindsight, and one's aspirations is their horizon and beyond. Our core-selves bestow upon the mind, body, and soul in the beauty of our contribution to our environment. Our thoughts, which are translated from the feelings we get from the soul are then transcribed into manifestation through speech and bodily language. If everything happens for a reason, then an independent variable should not be to question the moment's outcome. Regardless of how wide-spread or tall the dream is, the light from our soul should shine upon the masses. Every life is beautiful - such a statement is the origin to the "golden rule." Experiences amplify the beauty of life, more-so when those experiences are lessons from which we can learn, and then advised as testimonies. Experiences are in fact meant to be shared, and then interpreted in ways possible for developmental use.

This novella shows us the different perspectives from a community. It includes thoughts from the soul that can be manifested in due time according to experience. The forceful nature of our being is not of purity like a monochromatic dream. The reality may or may not bring the render into a vortex, but the goal nonetheless I want from you is to learn; to develop; to live. We as a species experience the moment, we learn—and as we learn we evolve. A wise man Lou Holtz once said, "In this world, you're either growing or you're dying so get in motion and grow." Hence, as we breathe, learning has its way of paving a path to that horizon we so seek.

I yearn you to learn, whether it may be through this book's message, through each line, or the kindle's burn from each experience you encounter. Moreover, I would like to add another wise man's words, Warren Buffet. He said, "The more you learn, the more you earn." What he forgot to add is the part where execution is behind the learning; taking the initiative to live out the experience is one's fulfillment to actually knowing. Experiences amplify the yearning of who I want to be. I hope in great confidence that reading this novella will allow the plant to grow exponentially from the mind's roots, for in turn, barriers will be overcome. Further, I have great confidence that the invigoration bestowed through these characters will resonate with your life's long story.

CHAPTER ONE

At 3:45AM Pacific Time, when anyone is least expecting a knock on their door or even a bang, Logan Powell's heart leaps out of his chest when he hears people break into his California home in West Hollywood. It was the LAPD escorting adults in white jackets, filtration masks and dark sun shades to cover their identity.

Blurred, Logan's vision is hindered as the bright lights are haywire, switching on and off throughout his living quarters. Alarms blared, Logan jumps out of his bed and into his slippers.

As he turns his neck sharply in an approximate 90 degree angle, there was a whiplash, almost causing him to render a vortex of memories to race through his mind in cyclical nature.

Footsteps stamping at each direction, Logan is perplexed on where to focus while the flickering lights are not making it easy. Unarmed, Logan is roughly corralled by estranged men unexpectedly.

"LET ME GO! LET ME GO!" Shouts Logan as his mouth is muzzled with a pair of hands.

His strength and determination gives him the will power to speak his mind at all costs. After being taken from his home in an abrupt, kidnap-like fashion, Logan snaps into liberation-filled ideas.

"If you resist one more goddamn time, we'll be forced to put you on the ground, dead or alive. Please cooperate," says the Officer as he calmingly demands Logan.

One of the Officers starts to stare at Dr. Powell. As these two have a staring contest, Logan was still on his computer chair located near the window in his bedroom. As Logan begun to inhale and then exhale at a relaxing pace, he was starting to take composite structure of his body and remain in full control.

He rescinds the built up strength. It was enough strength to use self-defense techniques when in hostile situations as such. Logan retreats back his anger and realizes he needs to have a cordial approach because he did not want to take that chance to be slain because of an issue he could have avoided.

Thank God I learned some self-control, he thought to himself. *That pride in the past would have made me a goner.*

Dr. Powell examines his actions as thoroughly as a psychiatrist analyzes their clients in genuine care. He senses the Military Police Officer's weary attitude, and he wonders why his emotions were built as high as New York City's World Trade Center until they came crumbling down from the profit of insurance-money-handling. *"Insurance-money-handling" is not a popular term, but speculation and deceit bestows the truth of that matter—a house of cards brought down by a demolition team.*

Distraught, disturbed and restrained –Dr. Powell wants answers along with his freedom, so he rightfully pores onto the Military Police Officer's uniform and cordially asks, "Can you please send your Commanding Officer in this New-York-City-sized bunker?"

The Officer was not an ignorant fellow himself and read the man he had physical strength over. *I could pound this guy in the face right now, but that was the old me*, he thought, standing in between the two sensor-powered sliding doors—commencing a brief pause.

Un-muzzled, after bestowing the utmost gratitude regarding the Officer's sense for hospitality, Logan asks,

"What's your name, son?" With veins popping from his forearm, Logan shows genuine interest in formal introduction.

The Officer slowly turns his head over his left shoulder and walks to the seated Logan. Although still restrained, he's able to firmly shake hands with an outstretched arm.

"Don't strain yourself now," says the Officer. "You'll only do harm to yourself."

With each step taken, a lesser shade of animosity is between the two. The Officer shook hands with Logan and they had become friends shortly thereafter, as he was drawn to Logan's aura.

As Dr. Logan Powell was done screening the Officer during their beloved handshake, there's a sensational thought: *Hmm, a man of changed circumstances, indeed. A man of improvement. I can surely resonate with that. A promising future.*

The Officer professionally responds, "I am David Martinez with the Corporal ranking division of the National Guard, specializing in delegated tasks to keep the human race for the strongest duration possible." He then continues politically and proudly, "I will see to it that our Commanding Officer gets here immediately." David, with his hands behind his back, in an arrested, restrained motion, walks away from Dr. Powell –and Dr. Powell shows an appealing expression, an enthusiastic one which grants friendship to his recipient.

"Great to have finally met you, Corporal Martinez, you show fine poise" says Logan.

"I've done some research on you," says Corporal Martinez says standing over Logan.

"Yeah? Found anything of interest?" replies Dr. Logan Powell.

"In fact, yes," says the Corporal chuckling. "You're a psychiatrist who's strapped in a chair."

"You humor me, David," blandly says Logan. "Although your perception of irony is rather tasteless, I could argue that you're a lonely Corporal who listened to the strapped and seated psychiatrist." Brief silence struck every angle of the room as Logan and David befriend one another at each one's sight.

"But it's only perception, right?" Logan asks rhetorically.

Each atom of energy, negative and positive, began manifesting on the basis of each one's perception.

On track with the objective, Corporal David retreats back to the sliding doors, leaving Dr. Logan Powell in his environment of silence.

• • •

The Commanding Officer walks in with his chest and chin aligned and pointed to Heaven. "Hello, sir; I am Commander Davis. What can I help you with?"

Dr. Powell, with his expertise in communication with human beings begins to look this tall fellow in the eye as he is respectfully approached.

"Well friend," Logan responds. "You can help me with a lot; first by kindly removing these restraints, then telling me what my next steps are."

"Certainly," says the Commander. "But with precaution. Baby steps, you know?"

"Understood," Logan agrees. "Carpe diem, huh?"

"Ha," chuckles the Officer in command. "Quite right, sir. Quite right."

"Well, I'm glad you agree because I would like for you to seize the moment and expedite this humorous entrapment."

Per respectful approach, it was as if there were no restraints on Dr. Powell's wrists whenever hands were shaken firmly, and with great honor.

Dr. Powell acknowledges this man as someone who envisions the upheaval of his ranks as a military police Officer to someone who is in command of his platoon— MP's and other personnel are dependent upon him to analyze their movements in subtlety.

"Commander, thank you for taking the time to come see me, but for starters, why am I restrained like a wild beast if I am being requested to help our human race on another planet approximately 21 light-minutes away, if I may add?" Logan asks in frustration.

Commander Davis sharply stares at Corporal Martinez with a dumbfounded look and asks "You told him!?" as he face-palmed himself in disappointment, shaking his head. "I wanted to tell him!" Jones shouts in envy.

Well, aren't I an asset, thinks Dr. Logan Powell, smirking. *This is a great sign.* Dr. Logan Powell realizes his value to this organization immediately Commander Davis gives way to his would-be intimidation tactic. This gives Logan great opportunity to have an upper hand in between the trifecta.

"Fellas, is this the schoolyard? Let's get on with the due-process, please," says Dr. Logan Powell, as his impatience increases before the two soldiers.

With no easy way to defuse the situation between the Corporal and Commander, Logan thinks quickly on his feet to refocus the attention on the matter at-hand.

"Gentleman, it is neither here nor there as to who or what informed me. I am going to Mars to be an asset, correct?"

"Yes," responds the Corporal and Commander in simultaneous format.

"Okay, so let's do what we must do and focus on the matter at-hand," says Logan, looking both men in the eye as he changes each syllable in each word.

The men respond with a nod in agreeance, but the two Officers look at each other in confusion on whether to inform Logan on another important matter. There was another elephant in the room, and Commander Davis steps in front of Corporal Officer Martinez to be on the 411-infantry team. He bestows the information in class-act fashion:

"Doctor, you may not know where you are located at this moment, but you are still on Earth. Your family has been contacted and they are receiving funds/assets which of course are under your name."

"That's quite all right," Logan cordially responds. "They will do what they have to do. I had almost always told them where to go if America's shit hits the fan—and hits it hard, with great impact."

Although the Commander gained a genuine connection with Logan, he proceeds to follow protocol. "We will need to let our doctors run some more examinations before the facility can release you from restraint; sincere apologies, Doc."

The Commander and Corporal Officer again were in sync with their motion toward the exit sign. But before they could leave, Dr. Powell shouted "Halt!" and chuckled, amused at militant's attentiveness to command.

The Commanding Officer and Corporal both look at each other distraughtly. Corporal Martinez excavates his emotions and rhetorically asks Commander Jones, "Is this Motherfucker serious?" He then takes a sharp turn, almost receiving whiplash.

"You are not military personnel; nor are you in any position to tell us 'halt!' Kidding or not, I do not want another would-be command out of your trap again."

Commander Davis places his right hand on Corporal Martinez's left shoulder, "May I kindly ask you to step away from Logan before things get ugly?"

As gears flip, Dr. Powell had become sincerely apologetic. "Sorry, guys, I honestly did not mean to offend you in any way. Please forgive me."

Both Officers look at each other and then at the white buffed tiles beneath their shiny black shoes. Then, in synchronized motion, gaze back at Dr. Powell making their way out the electric sliding doors.

"Come, Corporal," Commander Davis says. "We have important matters to attend."

Confused, Logan repeats after Jones as they are making way for departure of the room: "Important matters?" With resentment in his tone as they left, Dr. Logan Powell relinquishes the guard on his feelings like a levy to an overflow of water. "I thought I was important."

CHAPTER TWO

Dr. Powell sitting on a stainless steel chair made from Germany, did not let his emotions commingle with what he had as an assumption. His assumptions in the past would take him to the darkest of places, the trenches if you will—rock bottom. Dr. Powell tried his hardest to keep level headed, and eventually that's exactly what happened after he spoke with God. Logan Powell was raised in a monotheistic home. Although it was Lukewarm sometimes, he knew how to distract himself from negative energy.

Whenever a dispute would occur in the Powell household, his brain would react to share a solution he thought would be most beneficial for his family at that moment. As a young man, Dr. Powell had come to concurrence that family is everything it is supposed to be: loving, caring, supporting, encouraging, and strong.

As Dr. Powell is in a seated position, he is in very deep thought. Eyes closed, he visualizes himself as Le Penseur; The Deep Thinker. It was difficult, even for Dr. Powell to not go into his past. Being restrained tangibly in an enclosed room, he had never been. For he was, most of his childhood, enclosed and restrained from many things the world had to offer: lessons, language, and eminent skill. Although he had come to a perspective of everything, every gesture, every word spoken, every letter written happens for a reason, there was a lingering thought in his mind to revert back to how his parents raised him. As time had come to pass, there was little thought on the masses of blame to his upbringing.

He had learned to be alive in the moment—to be free. Every moment was cherished, and every moment to him, had resonated within his soul. Every experience he had gone through made him to be the person he is today: cordially sarcastic with a bit of spice; nonetheless a character.

• • •

Suddenly, there is a beeping sound indicating authorization to step into the same room as he. Dr. Powell looks up slowly and seems to notice a familiar face. "Susie?" Logan says, startled.

The woman looks Logan in the eye with deep meaning; with fire in her big brown eyes. Logan goes on to say, "Susie Campbell? Is that you?"

She flips her luscious hair dramatically and responds, "Dr. Susie Campbell to you, sir." Susie was trying to keep a stern face as best as possible.

Susie and Logan dated once before in High School, but then cut short because of differences and zero compromising during any minor disputes they may have had with each other. Hence, before any major disputes occurred, they looked after each other's mental health first—and sought asylum in their own pursuits to happiness.

Wearing a red dress and a white over-coat, hair tied into a bun, Susie was slowly walking, taking her time to get to Logan. A list of questions were erupting from each cell of her cerebrum. But instead, the questionnaire was imprinted in white ink illuminating from a pink sheet of paper on top of a German-made stainless steel clipboard, holding it vertically and across her left forearm. Logan distinctly observes Dr. Susie Campbell, as she is fiddling through papers before she dramatically looks Logan in the eyes.

They look at each other with great energy; on a colossal-like level. Each piece of energy took a quantum jump to the other person's mind without any manifestation.

"Hello, you must be Dr. Logan Powell. I am sorry for these restraints," she says remorsefully. "I will have them removed—"

Logan attempts to arrogantly interrupt, but Susie fires back quickly on her feet.

"Just as soon as we do more examinations to ensure you are not a threat to the environment and/or yourself. You will be released to the rest of the population headed to Mars—to a piece of land per your request, even before industrial development has started." Susie candidly continues, "I will just need to take some samples of your blood and urine -- and you shall be on your way to liberation."

"Something tells me that you say that to everyone," Logan says, as he regains his comfort with Susie Campbell.

The history of the two caused tension between their two dynamic brains; four hemispheres intertwined, but again, nothing was manifested. It was almost known of what their dialogue was interpreted as the two spoke in code.

Of her own powers, Dr. Susie Campbell releases Dr. Logan Powell from the restraints without following protocol.

Everyone in the enclosed population had their samples taken as they were seated.

Logan picks up on the gesture and relaxes himself into relief that everything was going to be alright at the end of the day. Faith instilled, it even made Logan deeply relaxes realizing she is not part of the sheep.

She is still the wolf beneath all the wool she disguised herself in.

As Logan finishes up to give her a urine sample, he couldn't help but think about his family and their whereabouts.

Although the trait to be worrisome was hereditarily from his mother, it did not hinder his prime focus on the live moment of handing the filled cup of urine to Dr. Campbell in steady motion, masking his momentary feeling.

"Thank you, Mr. Powell," says Dr. Susie Campbell.

"That's Doctor, Doctor," says Dr. Powell. "Just a friendly reminder."

"Touché," replies Susie. "I stand corrected."

She then took a small sample of blood by using a pin-like instrument, while putting it under an RB 50 Fluorescence Microscope details of the cells in-full.

"You were always good at Chemistry, Doc," Logan says in an attempt to start a normal conversation that would bring him to a vortex of their past time together, including a charming smirk.

Susie looks behind her right shoulder as her back is arches in a position over the stainless steel table, "Was that a way to start conversing, Logan?"

"Hmm, in-fact it was, Dr. Campbell."

"Well, it was a poor attempt," she says, trading a smirk with Logan, looking into the Microscope.

"You've been looking into that for quite some time now," Logan says out of curiosity. "Are you looking for a cure?"

Dr. Susie Campbell stands up-right and performs a 180 Degree turn responding, "A cure indeed … you just may have the formula to stop any plague."

Logan laughs out loud and Susie follows up with an illuminating smile of her own, which lights up Logan's soul.

As Logan and Susie start to reconnect within time, there is a rekindle with a slight breeze of wind attempting to prevent such reigniting from happening.

Being that there was no way for Susie to go to Mars the rest of the population, there were brief moments of silence during their conversation. All she could think about is when they would be able to see each other after he got sent off with the rest of the population; Susie has a duty to fill—as does Logan.

With little time to spare, Logan reaches over with his unrestrained hand and places it on her left shoulder. Heart racing, adrenaline pumping, Logan kisses Susie; Susie, relaxed, kisses him, as well. A fire ignites—and the only way to exhaust it would be with the use of the strongest water pressure from the facility's fire department.

Examinations are done and Logan wants to know about his family's welfare.

"I have a prerogative," says Logan.

"Yeah?" asks Susie. "Don't we all?"

"This is true," says Logan. "But I want to know if my family is alright."

Susie delighted him with a smile and briefly says, "They are perfectly fine."

Logan, not fond of that briefing, wants to learn more. He is a sponging all of the information possible, gathering clues to solve a mystery.

Chapter THREE

As Logan and Susie part ways, they themselves were confident that it would only be temporary before they make contact again. With the help of faith and strong belief system, Logan kept his head up remembering one of his favorite hip-hop artists: Tupac Shakur.

Music has more often than not been a part of Logan's life--from the appreciation of a fine melody played by the illustrious pianist Yiruma based out of Japan to the lively abundance-filled music played by the church choir during his formative years.

Although there would be no music being played at Logan's current tangible setting, his imagination of violins and pianos melodied—serenating his mind, which in turn hands him the gift of security to happiness and contentment.

Intuitively, Logan closes his eyes and thinks to himself. *Any given situation could turn out to be worse than what it may seem. Hence, in every dark cloud there is a silver lining.*

Logan is walking down the halls in the unknown base with two Military Policemen—a part of the National Guard.

Positioned on the west-wing of the facility, they are on overnight patrol.

Suddenly, an alarm wails through the corridors as the three men are walking to their destination: a courtyard with the rest of the population. It is described to be a courtyard inside a huge, secretly modern facility on the west side of Texas.

"Someone was trying to escape, but it is thankfully handled," another MP blares over the radio.

"We have a rebel on our hands, don't we, gentlemen," Logan condescendingly chimes in. "Or maybe a whistleblower?"

As a child, Logan was rebellious in nature—both at home and school. With technology at his fingertips, Logan was an explorer and a sponge for knowledge. Often awareness prompted his understanding that there was something more to life than poverty.

In comparison to those in his living quarters, Logan's family was blessed with food, clean water and consistent shelter.

It is imperative for Logan to help facilitate his family's upbringing to success—not for society, but for future generations, testimonials and himself.

Dr. Powell is susceptible to change—an open book to new people and ideas. Adapting affirmatively to the manifestations of his environment, Logan becomes vulnerable to learning new perspectives and cultures.

Working harder and smarter has frequently resonated with Logan as he developed to become a man—and to know thyself.

Lord knows and bestowed it upon one point; someone must be leader and display it as an example in glass that is shined everyday day for transparency. Reap what you sew, and so shall you reap the benefits which are birthed from the labor that makes the soul vibrant.

Communication is consistently keen, sharp as a katana's blade finessed by Honjo Masamune.

Logan arrives to the rest of the population and is astonished by the plethora of people, mostly 21-37 and of diversification. Logan, 27 years of age, and turning 28 in the coming months, feels as though the people amongst him are portrayed to be people of importance—and people of sacrifice.

He surveys the area and makes an exertion to search for family, as he was starts to wander again. His train of thoughts grope his mental capacity to extreme places; a setting that only consists of a climax and an on-going resolution. It was a place of insanity; a place where he did not call home.

What Dr. Logan Powell calls home is being surrounded by people he unconditionally adored—and that of nature which is reciprocated. Logan agreeing with his consciousness, comes into a revelation out loud: "Family is everything." With a tone of resentment, "They never get left behind."

Removing Logan from an element of nostalgia, a man approaches Logan and greets him like a host from a boutique hotel.

"Hello, sir!" Yelps the greeter.

"Hi," responds Logan. "You derailed me from my train of thoughts. Are you an Amtrak Conductor?"

Logan corrects his mannerism and reiterates, "I'm sorry. I need to concentrate."

"No problem," says the greeter, handing Logan a pamphlet. "Have a wonderful day."

"And you, sir," replies Logan.

"Thank you!"

Dumbfounded, Logan is battling his thoughts: The family of his is being trumped by strings of which attached the kiss from Dr. Susie Campbell as a would-be genuine connection.

Logan retracts from his cerebrum to puzzle his shattered mind.

"Ugh," Logan grunts as he holds his nasal bridge tightly while closing his eyes with his head down.

The greeter rushes to Logan. "Are you okay, sir?"

"Yes, I'm fine, I'm fine. Thank you," says Logan. "Run along now let me think."

Although there was a connection on her end, as well, Susie was informed she needed to slip a pill into Dr. Logan Powell so that there would be no memory of how he had gotten to the main population. While walking to the main population with the Military Police, he was actually put on a cart unconscious of his surroundings.

The people who he thought to be MP's were two scientists trying to hold Logan Powell together. There was a fight which had burst through the shiny hallways on their way to the population of soon-to-be space-traveling migrants.

Logan's focus is to remove himself from the restraint he saw himself in. He feels as constricted as a snake's prey, but oppositely breathing steadily.

Logan, in the deepest thought possible, relies on faith and subconscious feelings. He repeatedly thinks to himself, *I'll be fine and I'll prosper*. His faith surpasses all doubt of his removal from the chains of which he sought to unlock to his freedom.

One of the scientists, out of courage and guilt, surrenders the need for a tough act. She surrenders herself to Logan and embraces the truth-bearing reaction to her action made.

After Logan surveys the area from a platform above the main floor, he looks to the right and there was Susie. "Logan, I have something important to tell you," says Susie, anxious to release from her mind what a huge burden on her shoulders and body was.

She realizes that she had done something wrong and felt the imperative feeling to apologize. "Logan, I slipped a pill down your throat when we kissed and made out." As guilty as she feels, Susie's hands were covering her face in disgrace; she could not believe what she had done.

Logan replies, "It is okay, Susie. I knew that you slipped the pill." Logan grabbed her arms and looked her in the eyes. "I understood the repercussions of the ordeal, and I am a depressed man without my family, so having something to calm my nerves worked well—even more so since I do not take any pills to calm my nerves. My family and faith are my cure and without those factors, I am a product of nothing."

"That's very sweet, Logan," candidly says Susie.

"Thanks, Susie. My kids are awesome--and so is my wife, she--"

"Your wife!?" Susie interrupts.

"Yes, Dr. Campbell, she is awesome, the best human being to ever have treated me correctly, who loves me for me," Logan answers.

Susie fixes herself out of her vulnerable state. She sniffles, bringing back the waterfall of tears that were going to trickle down her cheeks after learning that Logan is married with children. She looks at his left hand for confirmation of marriage—and she notices he actually has the gold band gripping his finger.

 Logan wears his ring everywhere he goes; it never gets taken off. Evident to him never taking the ring off, one could see from a plain view a bright red mark, distinguishing man from boy.

The men and women in Logan's family and circle of trust are role models—and so he took after them and their ethical ways, as did Plato to Socrates.

They lead by example and passed that trait down to Dr. Logan Powell. Family-orientation is important to Logan, and although Logan's family is not near him, he knows where his heart lies. It is in the hands of the Spiritual being who is soulful.

Life continues, so Logan and Susie part ways … yet again. "Till next time, Dr. Campbell." They shake hands and both bow down in respect to each other's presence. If Logan had eyes in the back of his head, he would focus his vision on Susie's departure.

But instead, he focuses on the moment at-hand and back to the man who approaches him, greets Logan as if he were the host soon to escort Dr. Powell to his seat. *All he needed was a podium and clipboard to match the uniformed actions he performed,* thinks Logan.

Logan's focus on the moment made him appreciative of the man and his approach—they both firmly shake hands while looking at each other in the eyes. Logan knew of respect and a good first impression stuck with him through the long-hall. Dr. Logan Powell lets the man break the ice: "I am the first one here in attendance; can you believe that?"

"Actually, I can," Logan responds condescendingly. Smiling at the man, Logan is performing a class-act show bid.

Logan had grown up around peers that he was not able to trust. It is second-nature for the Doctor to sometimes manipulate people's minds with his genuinely kind gestures.

Most assured, faith in this man being of importance to Logan's life is not so apparent—especially after learning about Susie immediately putting on her wool coat for the sake of security.

Logan, with his mind trained to swiftly move forward, does not show any signs of grudge—only a force field surrounding his physical body protecting him from any demonic spirit that may lay upon any of his atoms, rebuking any negative energy that may have taken a quantum leap into his direction.

"We best stick together; this whole colonization thing is surreal," says the man.

While still shaking each other's hands for five seconds, Logan felt as if he was in a corporate/shareholders meeting preparing to lobby for a politician. In Logan's mind, it is too often that there are many humans with ulterior motives and are not genuine, so Dr. Logan Powell is prepared to take his interactions as politically as possible.

"Okay, that is about enough. I have not gotten your name, sir," says Logan, as he stands upright and eagle-eyes the suspicious host of captured people.

Logan turns upright into a power stance and takes control of the encounter, attempting to make the man nervous.

The man lowers his posture and softly says his name … "Monty."

Monty, just like the other 2.998 human being; were chosen for a purpose. Although their trip may involve death sooner than anticipated in their earlier lives, their journey to civilization on another planet will have a degree of difficulty to survival of astronomical level.

Their purpose will be their own personal goal to achieve when making a mark on a planet approximately 21 light minutes away with current technology. They understand that amongst them is a predicament to do better for their future generations.

For they will sacrifice their own lives to make the universe a traveling-accessible universe; some may call them heroes, some may call them a blessing—nonetheless, it was not an environment of worrisome behavior which made it peaceful. Monty comes from South Africa, a young man who had also gotten pulled from his living quarters.

Monty's living arrangements were not like Logan's: Monty lived in a village, where he and his family practiced religion and were hardworking people making an honest buck. As Monty figured he was chosen for a purpose, there was no stopping him to reach his life's calling.

As a young boy, Monty would every day gaze up at the stars amongst him, wondering about the cosmos that seemed to be very close to him. The stars aligned perfectly at times, and at other times, novas began to emerge. They formed an artistic presence, something so powerful and beautiful, it made Monty's father cry beside him. Monty was brought up to appreciate the nature around him, including the moment. 'Carpe diem' they would call it; there was never an urge to keep his day at a pause and keep the doors that were awaiting to be open--because eventually they will close. Monty's father, in good faith, spoke of timely initiative.

Time waits on not an atom; change is inevitable; Monty and his dad witnessed that, as they saw the stars create explosion, there was a supernova that existed—which surpassed their horizon of ever being present in the moment. Their moment was the horizon; they saw the galaxy form something unexplainable--something only witnessed beings get the chance to either appreciate God's work or take for granted His presence in the universe and all the other galaxies millions of light-years away. Monty was there with a divine purpose; and his purpose was be rich in wellness with the stars in the Milky Way and beyond.

"Pleased to meet you, Monty. I did not intend to approach with an unwelcoming attitude," Logan says cordially, finally embracing the younger man. "I do not begin to trust people I have no recollection of."

"No need to justify, sir. I understand," responds Monty with a smile from one brother to another. Friendship began. Logan then turns his attention to the crowd of people and put both his hands behind his back, with great posture, his right hand on top of his left. With his eyes closes, he pictures a great deal of the future if we had more Montys in the world. Logan then put his right hand on Monty's left shoulder to embrace the colonization on a different planet light minutes away. Unconsciously, Logan helps facilitate Monty's courage to an upheaval.

"You are right, two minds are certainly better than one during an adventure, and maybe you are an omen in my life."

Intrigued, Monty asks, "An omen, you say?"

"Yeah, that's right, kid," Logan responds, excited from Monty's curiosity.

"What's that?" asks Monty.

Logan smirks and puts his hand on Monty's left shoulder, and says "You have a lot to learn, my friend."

"And so do you ... Logan, is it?" Monty replies, looking Logan in the eye, hoping that he can solidify a bond.

Monty is not a miserable being, but he relishes company—he enjoys an environment that he could learn from.

Sparkled with wonder, Monty is starting to view Dr. Logan Powell as a role model. Monty never had that role-model figure in his life, so as he begins to build more rapport with Logan, their frequency starts to ignite like a kindle.

"Let me show you around, but first, you tell me what an omen is," says Monty as his curiosity reignites his the fire to learn from his mentor.

Inhaling deeply, Logan spews his deep thoughts and says, "You will know, as it will organically approach you on your path to your calling in this universe. You will know as you continue to reach your turning point in life."

"What's a turning point?"

"Are you familiar with a story climax chart?"

"No, sir." Monty's eyes started to widen. Anxiety from Monty starts to become apparent--his blood is rushing and is eager to learn what Logan has to teach him.

"In your life, right now, Monty you are in an exposition, as am I," says Logan. "We begin with an exposition and rising action as we lead up to a climax, which is the turning point in our lives."

Monty is surely satisfied with Logan's answer. Little does Logan know, he has a quick learner standing before him, "So is our interaction an omen?"

Logan sharply looks Monty in the eye and does not exchange any words. There is a crossroads of microbiology and the universe during Logan's thought process.

He resonates with Monty as the question arose, like how a plant arises from the concrete. Dr. Logan Powell was the light being shone upon Monty's energy. Their telepathy connects, and Logan not expecting that to occur, is vulnerable from the array of beaming light.

Arms crossed, "Hmm," Logan replies.

Both Monty and Logan were raised in monotheistic households, but he was Muslim which was perfectly accepted and loved by Logan. Although Logan and Monty had come from two different cultures, they embrace each other like agape love. Logan, filled with satisfaction, is aware he has someone looking up to him as a mentor. Logan was not expecting Monty to catch on as fast as he had done.

Logan views Monty as a prodigy. As moments pass by, "The River Flows in You" by Yiruma begins to play in the mind of Logan's. With the tight correlation of the sweet serenade from Yiruma's finger tips pressing the ivory keys of his Yamaha U1 piano. Logan's perspective to see growth is aligned with music for the soul. Growth is fascinating.

Oddly, he says out loud to Monty as his thoughts are laid out with a melody, "Music is a moral law, Monty. It gives soul to the universe, wings to the mind, flight to the imagination, and charm and gaiety to life and to everything."

"Wow…," Monty says in amazement, lost for words.

"Do you know who said that, champ?" Logan asks.

"No," replies Monty. "I was hoping you'd give me a reference before spewing out a philosophical quote."

"In fact, it was Plato, an Athenian philosopher who shared that with the world," affirmatively says Logan.

As growth is an overture of evolution, Logan thinks, *it correlates with resolution to oneself. Monty is extraordinary—his energy gives off love and curiosity. Humility is what he shows. I will live in the moment with Monty, and we'll both see the journey of life together as he begins to embed any information I may bestow upon him.*

Monty proceeds to show the quarters of the area where the abundant amount of people were. As Logan was not surprised, he notices that there was segregation between the different complexions and classes of people. He was still surveying the area in search of his family that he was yet to get news about. Curiosity struck Logan's mind running at one million strides per minute--and the question arose: "Where is your family, Monty?"

Monty replies with his head down, "I do not have a family." There was a sudden pause between the two.

"Well, you have no worries, huh?" Logan asks candidly with humorous intentions.

Ignoring the questions, Monty becomes curious of Logan's family. Logan could feel his urge to close off the kid by just walking away or changing the subject on the matter that made him feel uncomfortable at the moment. He reverts back to the genuine feeling he had gotten from Monty as their frequency had gotten stronger as time spent together grew from the root of universal love. With a calm expression, Logan responds, "I'm in search of them, buddy. I haven't a clue where they may be."

"Maybe I can facilitate the issue and help out," Monty brainstorms.

"You are very kind, Monty. Thank you. I will keep you informed if we should work together on such a specific path after I fully survey each quarter before it is time to take our voyage to Mars."

With disparity clinging to Monty's interpretation on Logan's no need for help, his posture curves into a wide parabola. "Take your time, friend..."

As Logan takes a stroll to search for his family, the stroll itself hinders his faith.

Logan briefly speaks to God requesting reassurance and counsel for the strength he needs to persevere through any human's toughest battle; their mind. As the perseverance was underway, there was nothing that could put him at halt, for he will break down any barrier of negativity, so he can proceed to the following quarter of the populated area.

Nonchalantly, Logan walks the courtyard to get food from the only place to get food from: a fruit bar. Logan reaches in his pocket instinctively and pulls out a wad of cash to purchase fruit for him and Monty—to eat harmoniously.

"Where did this come from?" he asks himself out loud standing in line at the fruit bar.

"From the greatest giver of all," says a stranger in line.

"Are you a believer?" asks Logan.

"A believer in what?" responds the stranger.

"A believer in the truth and the light of –"

"Oh, hold that thought. Getting fruit," the man says, interrupting Logan.

"Sure," Logan calmly responds.

"All right," says the man, looking Logan in the eyes cradling his fruit with two arms. "What were you trying to tell me? –Something about truth and light?"

"Quite right," says Logan. "Something about truth and light; that of which dilutes the nature of man who may be spreading themselves too thin."

A fruit drops from the man's arms. "Ah, case in point, my friend," says Logan. "You want to enjoy the fruits of your labor, but you seem to be carrying too much."

Resentment in the man's tone, "Not really."

"Oh?" says Logan. "Whomever I believe in helps me to carry belongings in a balanced fashion."

"That's good for you," responds the man. "But, it is also food for thought. You see, I think I know where you're getting at before you provide me a filibuster," blandly says the man.

"Where's that, brother?" Logan asks, genuinely curious.

"Well, to keep things short and sweet like the apple which fell from my branch of an arm, I'm an atheist."

"Interesting," says Logan caressing five-o'clock shadow on his chin.

"Indeed," agrees the man. "Listen, I have to get goin'. See you around, sir. Thank you for the spoken word."

"Pleasure," says Logan. *A seed sewn,* thinks Logan as the man finally walks away after finally attaining a basket for his fruit.

Meanwhile, during the dialogue a line has been held up, and people were in-tune, eavesdropping.

Logan, noticing the attention spewed onto his momentary conversation, says, "I don't blame you for listening in on two perspectives. I love being human."

Logan and Monty have themselves a fresh batch of fruit, which consists of granny-smith apples, pears, mangoes, pineapple, strawberries and bananas.

"A nice delicatessen, Logan!" shouts Monty in excitement.

Echoing his energy, Logan responds, "Amen!"

The administrative team that is in control of the operation strongly believes in the depiction of bodily temples. Their top priority is health and wellness. Not only is everyone in a trance of getting to planet Mars— they are important people to society.

The 3,000 people rendered as a population is in the cusp of utopia and social classes. The division of the people are on a bell-curve, and the parabolic shape shifted more to the right of the derivative than usual. A diversity of people helps balance out each percentile of human expectations. Of the 3,000 people, 2,000 are expected to meet expectations, 500 to exceed, and the other 500 to be obsolete in their journey to survival.

This is not one's ordinary confinement. It consists of several windows of opportunity to obtain fruit, but none to obtain nature's sun-lit skies and grounds. Behind health and wellness being a top priority was an opportune moment to make Earthly Martians a group of different races and ethnicities. No matter your skin color, there was divine opportunity to uphold citizenship on the red planet.

Logan, even with eyes of caution at this unknown facility, is in fact a feminist and believes that all people should be equal. He highly praises a society of equal rights, which includes diversity and the golden rule. His intentions are to live amongst integrity, ethics, and faith. Dr. Logan Powell finds the colonization of Mars to be interesting—there is not just one race or skin color being chosen to perform the diverse and interracial power the world so desperately needs to obliterate racism as a whole.

"Give me a few minutes, Monty," says Logan as he unusually looks over Monty's shoulder.

"Take your time," replies Monty as he takes a chomp into the ripe apple.

Logan then went on to a gentlemen who looks awfully familiar. Walking near his presence, Logan, smears the apple's juice he had laying on his cheek from the huge bite he had taken.

Nonchalant and cordial, Logan approaches the man. The man senses a strange feeling from Logan's energy and begins to focus on each step toward his physical being—as if a quantum jump of electromagnetic frequency leaned forward to discover the aura Dr. Powell laid upon the man ten feet away and closing.

Logan, outspoken, waves out to the man and asks out loud, "Hey, my friend, do I know you?"

The man looks at Logan with a gruesome facial expression and did not nudge to change it due to the peculiar nature of Logan's approach.

Logan goes on in a cordial manner and asks, "Well, would you like to tell me your name?"

"Sure, my name is Jermaine… Jermaine Jones," the man says nervously.

"No need to be startled, my friend," Logan responded with a smirk on his face. "I thought you may have been someone who is a part of my family."

"But never mind that, Logan says, abruptly switching the subject. "Jermaine Jones, huh? That's a catchy name, and one that I will be sure to remember."

"Are you being condescending?" asks Jermaine.

Condemned, Logan responds, "Not at all, son."

"Don't call me son," sharply says Jermaine. "Who are you searching for anyway?"

"My home," responds Logan.

"I can resonate with that," says Jermaine. "My home is most assuredly not a physical place, but my family of which I've parted from."

Before Logan was able to provide empathy the man proceeds, "Do you have a name, guy?"

"I thought you'd never ask," responds Logan.

Jermaine's conversing buddy immediately stands upright, with his hands at hip, boastfully introducing himself and says, "My name is Dr. Logan Powell."

"It is clear to me that you are very proud of what you have become," says Jermaine. "So you found your calling … that's awesome. Good for you, my friend."

Logan then smiles at the man in acceptance for his words. "Much obliged, brother."

"May I ask—?" Logan asks in an attempt to provide sympathy in response the man's downward body language.

Interrupting Logan, the man scoffs, "Don't need your sympathy, dude."

"I'm all ears," says Logan. "I'm here for a reason, so would you rather talk or be given a piece of advice based on an assumption."

"I'll take the advice," says the man. "But after, I need to be left alone to think."

"Fair enough, Mr. Jones," says Logan, respectfully. "I know not of what you may be in search of, but be that as it may, we are all in search of meaning. Although my calling has been found, and it has been received fondly, I still am not aware of what the meaning of this current interaction is going to produce. You and I, we are factors of an everlasting environment with connections because each moment we share with each other is timeless—it can never be dismantled from the Universe's attraction. Simply put, champ, whatever battles that may go on in your head, give way and end the war. I will end my filibuster with this quote from Plato."

Logan closes his eyes and recites the quote as he reads each word from the drapes of which block the tangible vision to his environment, "Only the dead have seen the end of the war."

"Thank you, Doctor," responds Jermaine.

"My pleasure, sir."

Chapter FOUR

Dr. Powell feels important to his community of people, especially since he learned of the opportunity to go to Mars is going to be the mission, but he was still unsure of when their departure would be. Mind in shambles, he is unsure of many things from past to future, but acclimating himself into the calling to help people is his personal dream manifesting before his eyes.

Although hardship seeks to test Dr. Powell's ability to focus on the task at-hand for humanity, he is in no obligation to fall by the wayside. With faith on a bright horizon, family, love and peace is in his purview.

The year is 2022 and Dr. Powell is cognizant of the technologies the government obtained from private venture companies, some of which are present in the facility.

Capitalism? Logan questions to himself.

Everyone wants to make their mark on the Big Red Planet, which boasts to be very similar to Earth, according to Earthly scientists' findings.

Human beings have the natural ability to explore; once there is a mountain in sight there is a natural instinct to overcome such a tangible obstacle to see what is on the opposite side. The climax is usually endured with at least minimal hardship, but there tends to be two types of people in this universe—ones who are strong enough to persevere and weather the storm, and those who will fold under pressure.

Humans in this day-and-age in this facility are like coal: they bestow energy and when under pressure, they shine brightly like a diamond and are stronger than ever. For future generations to come, the majority of people, if not all, will have their names remembered as one of the first group of human beings to cultivate civilization beyond our stratosphere and beyond orbit on the Earth-like planet, Mars.

• • •

As for the population of the facility, they have an ultimatum: preserve their DNA—their physical body or take off in the readily available Galactic Hopper provided by the private sector and their delegations in twelve months.

Months of training will include induced blood, sweat, and tears: the training is essentially to fast forward astronaut training. For those departing Earth as settlers to-be, the pressure is on. The foundations of which they will lay, will be the foundation of the human species in continuum.

The population includes all sorts of ethnicities and career backgrounds relevant to the mission toward Mars, approximately 21 light minutes away. Some of the people excavated includes those who were pulled away from their family for scientific experimentation in accordance to their own willful permission to be extracted from their homes.

With the government having orchestrated this ordeal, there is nothing that the supposed oppressed could do. Moreover, there is nothing that could have been done prior to their arrival because of signed agreements to depart at any time the government sees fit to their schedule.

Military Police Officers raided homes all over the world and had in-mind to utilize many of these people as assets to the proposed mission: colonize Mars. A government cannot function without its social hierarchy in place—and for such a factor to essentially be in place, there must be a fine line between societal views: socialistic, communistic and capitalistic. All three views, which do not limit to the total, create segregation. So long as there is segregation, there will be oppression. There cannot be oppression without repression.

Repression tends to be regression at the unknown facility, primarily within the population. Logan and others could notice people who were in close proximity to being as ballistic as Atomic bombs exploding on celestial landscapes.

Dr. Logan Powell, a natural mediator, accepts his role on Earth, as he will plant a fresh seed of morality and service to the people of his community.

Being a mender into social conflict, Logan puts the people at a stage of comfort. At-ease, his posture indicates his natural element of rising above obstacles like David to Goliath.

Skills of his that translate into being a profound communicator and connector brings him closer to people; it helps the foundation of which he so chooses to mold like clay.

As he gains familiarity with Monty's personality, trust begins to form, which thus includes a foundation of stone—a diamond-like foundation. The parameters of the stone consisted of a symmetrical area that formed like water which can be reflected by light that gives a gravitating nature.

They mold their relationship based on honesty—and that is the only factor from the foundation they need.

• • •

There is a rattle on the loudspeaker, and it is the Commander's voice sounding the news of full occupancy along the facility which all the travelers were held. "Hello, everyone—we have reached our full capacity of three thousand people for our mission." Logan listens carefully, "I know some of you may be worried about your families, but I assure you that they are well-taken care of."

"Well, isn't that just dandy," sarcastically says Logan, gaining attention. "What a relief, right?" Logan searches around for confirmation, but all he could find was Monty standing by his side.

"Don't worry, Logan," says Monty. "Trust the process."

Murmurs start to flow through the crowd, and there are so many butterflies within the group body, that even caterpillars would be overwhelmed.

The Commander continues to speak, but in cordiality and satire, "I'm sure some of you have heard the rumor of an ultimatum because some guards can never stick to a code."

In spite of a friendly way of speaking to the enclosed population, the Commander keeps a mental note of the corporal private. Still seated, without staring at the soldier, the Commander sharply mutes the microphone and says, "Treason."

The soldier's heart drops to his stomach. Such word is not welcoming in any shape, way or form. With a heart of his own, the Commander thinks to strike down upon the men under his confided regime when disobeying orderly code, but he did not enforce anything this time.

"Let this be a warning, private," says the Commander towering over the accused party of treason.

"Yes, Commander," respectfully replies the private corporal.

"At-ease," says the Commander.

The Commander makes note of how frequently one shall push his buttons before he takes action to induce punishment upon thee. The corporal private thinks to

himself: *How could he have known?* He then looks around
the command post and spots one of his fellow soldiers
snickering after the announcement. The soldier then
questions the loyalty of his comrade, a fellow to the
organization he is a part of.

As the announcement adjourns, Commander Davis
stands upright from his seat and slowly walks toward the
corporal private's direction, giving him a smirk. Such smirk
indicates that although he was put in the spotlight, there is
something that needed to be done—a form of discipline that
forges his mind not to worry about his status as a ranking
member of the Military community.

Commander Davis touched the private's right
shoulder with his left hand and walked past him to speak
with the peanut gallery—the snickering soldier. "What's
funny, soldier?"

The Soldier stands up-right with his hands to his side,
parallel to his pockets, with his chin up. The Commander
leans forward to the soldier's left ear, with his hands behind
his back, speaks lowly but does not whisper: "It's only a
man's name, right?"

Clearing his throat, Commander Davis regains his
posture and says, "At-ease, soldier. Head down to the

community where you will find people to speak with, instead of gossiping."

"Yes, sir," replies the soldier in a condemning fashion.

"After I make my final announcement for the day, see to it that connections and relationships have been built to better your people skills" says the Commander, as he makes his way back to the seat where the microphone is placed before him.

With half of the population staring up into a speaker, it is only imaginable for those to envision the expression of the Commander as he was making announcements, which attained to everyone. The other half displayed comfortability and show confidence in their will to exceed humanity's expectations to further life in a celestial body.

Speaking amongst themselves with positivity and bearing fruit from the intellectual dialogue that was genuinely put forth, the vow to manifest their thoughts into tangible being. Speaking of plans and of great certainty for humanity is at the cusp of their energy-filled conversations.

As the pause comes to an end, there a loud beeping sound, indicating to the population a notice that the Commander is going to speak.

"We will conduct two lines for a huge decision you will need to make very soon." There is an assembly being formed adjacent to the population at-hand within the same area of the facility. Soldiers from the facility begin working to help form this line with two black ropes that include brass stations leading to kiosks.

Suddenly, a loud force which echoes the room: "THE TIME STARTS NOW," states Commander Davis. "Please, at your own leisure, make your way to either window where it reads 'Registration.' You will then choose your division wisely. Remember, first come; first serve." With genuine candor, Commander Davis says, "Good luck and God bless."

Dr. Logan Powell, with sarcastic gestures, salutes the speaker. Logan then speaks to himself, "Thank you for at least showing your face."

With the salute, attention followed him. There were several people in a ten-foot radius from Logan who nodded his direction in respect to being grounded. "Very valiant, I'd say," Logan says, not noticing the eyes looking toward his direction. As Logan ends the snarky remarks toward

Commander Davis, he is still standing upright—no one looking around him is familiar with Dr. Logan's character, so they respect his outside appearance from afar which bestows confidence and bravery.

Dr. Logan Powell looks up with humility and candor, respecting the Commander. Grateful for being given the unique opportunity for migration to Mars. In five seconds time, contemplation, Dr. Logan Powell makes a firm decision.

Closing his eyes in gratuitous nature, Logan is beside himself, in his own world, he is in oblivion to anyone else's thoughts—in the moment.

Suddenly, there is a tug from a young man, looking up at Dr. Powell. With this tug followed a sincere request of prayer upon his voyage. Logan is confused, but in awe and smiles at the young man.

His stature depicts someone as spiritual, or the young man may have heard through the grapevine of Dr. Logan Powell's enlightened nature.

Logan places his right hand in the young man's shoulder. Logan, with previous experiences on having God speak through him to others, had never come across a request until this instant. Logan, still in awe, and in the moment, drops down to one knee and covered his face, almost as if he were 'Tebowing,' when in-fact Tim Tebow is not nostalgic in the least. Dr. Logan Powell—he is not much of a fan of American Football. Rather, a sign of respect and admiration.

Finally, with all the spiritual guidance and strength collected from Logan, words manifest from Dr. Powell's mouth to this young gentleman. "Son, repeat after me …"

The young man fixes his posture—as straight as a condemned soldier in the presence of his commander. The young man standing up straight before Logan Powell shows anything other than mediocrity—he shows courage; he shows valor; he shows bravery; he shows boldness. Logan respects the young man.

Logan then continues with his eyes closed to speak to the young man with the spiritual presence still fresh between the two human bodies:

"I will be safe with the grace of God. I know that He will never leave me, nor will He forsake me. As long as I have faith that Jesus will be present for any support that I need, I will prosper in fruitful energy that I can bestow unto the world. As my light will be shone m upon thee, I will illuminate the dark and prepare for everything we thought one day would unimaginable. Thank you God—in your blessed name we pray: Amen."

"Amen," says the young gentleman, repeating after Dr. Logan Powell.

After their eyes open, they connect with one another. Logan then realizes that the boy was not going to repeat everything word that was spoken in harmony. Both smile— the light is illuminated and faith is restored within the young man.

Although Logan requested the young man to repeat after him, the young man listens and after agreeing with the prayer from Logan's spirit, he wisely says, "We have two ears to listen and one mouth to speak."

Dr. Logan Powell looks at the young man with solidarity and praises him for the sagacious words. The young man then continues and says, "So I used more of what I have for the greater good to let you speak for us both."

Logan responds, "Thank you, kid."

The energy that connects them both has come into an electronic force neither of them can fathom. Logan rises, looking at the boy in the eyes and still in disbelief of the courage and bravery he shows.

Logan squats down like a baseball catcher ready to embrace pitches which would reach upwards of one hundred miles per hour. In such moment, Logan is the catcher and the young man is the ball coming full speed ahead.

"Hey, kid... what's your name?" Logan curiously asks.

"My name is Santiago... Santiago Del Valle," he replies.

There is a slight pause between Logan and Santiago. A pause of Deja Vu; Logan remembers this moment—the significance of manifesting literal common grounds with the young man on the electric wheelchair.

Logan is astonished within the moment. Not only were the energetic frequencies between the two human beings of a parallelogram, but there was a nostalgic thought which vividly flowed through the mind of Dr. Logan Powell.

"Do you believe in Deja Vu, Santiago?" asks Logan, looking into the young man's eyes while holding on to an arm-rest from the chair. The chair is of chrome-plated finishing, which includes premium leather seating. Logan, being familiar with the leather, figured such chair was produced in Europe for Santiago's ergonomic preference.

Santiago, with eyes glittering as bright as the moon in the starry night sky, faces Logan and leans forward, "Yes, sir. I do."

"I believe that this occurrence happened for a colossal purpose, my friend," Dr. Powell says.

"This moment of Deja Vu that occurred has confirmed that you and I are on the correct path to greatness within our lives," says Dr. Logan Powell beginning to feel the energy within his body flaring. It is ready to bestow the light he has and shine it as bright as the Sun itself. He stands up, towering the physically disabled young man on the chair.

"This moment is our moment, so let's continue this journey—the best journey—and let's plant our seeds of fruitful work!" Logan says intending to motivate his recipient.

Logan bows his head and thinks to himself humbly. Graciously he thinks, *Thank You for this moment, and let Your will be done. Amen.*

The boy subsides from tears trickling down his cheeks and reaches out to Logan's hand. Logan grabs Santiago's hand with both hands in gratuity for a humane share in the moment of energetic fire. Flames scorching so highly, lukewarm temperature would never be able to coincide.

"It was a pleasure to have met you, son," Logan says in sincere nature. "I have to go now."

"Maktub!" replies the young man in excitement.

Logan, in awe, smiles at the boy. Chuckling in admiration. The boy laughs, too.

They both will remember this moment, as it was a moment meant to stick—it is meant to embed; it is meant to be seen. To be looked upon as an example of love.

Logan and Santiago tangibly part ways, but their spiritual connection is of ripe nature—they both savored every nutrient which filled their mind, body, and soul.

Logan does not know what's on the young man's mind, but he looks over his shoulder watching Santiago return to the friends he had made. There are gestures of wonders and immense curiosity. Santiago looks to be articulating his experience because his testimony is relatable to that of his fleet.

Tuning in from afar, Logan notices people amongst him are surrounding his good nature. Two men are calmly seated with their legs crossed, along with a man and woman at their sides. A circle was formed as they are listening to Santiago speak of fruitful bearings.

With the spiritual connection relatively strong, Logan has faith in Santiago speaking to the group and leading them to the greater paths with his evolved wisdom. As he hopes to see Santiago in the future, Logan smiles feeling that Santiago hopes for the same.

Dr. Logan Powell turns his head in a ninety degree motion and looks over his left shoulder as Monty is patiently waiting to be spoken to, as well.

"Monty, were you present this whole time?" Logan asks, surprised.

"I was drawn to the illumination you and the gentleman shared. There was a burst of light and fire which dignified liberation through the mind, body, and soul," Monty replies in exhilarated but nervous fashion. He places his right hand over his left forearm, and Logan could not help but notice the humility displayed by Monty, a friend.

Dr. Logan Powell then raises his left hand onto Monty's crown. Monty bows his head and closes his eyes. His eyelashes causes a small air pocket as they close fast and shut tight. His eyes craving for the liberation he so desperately yearns, Monty envisioned greatness as he and Dr. Logan Powell both pray together in harmony.

He envisions a fusion; similar to a bond between two Super Saiyans from Dragon Ball Z, a Japanese anime show.

Monty, in his truest form, coincides with personal growth and is aware that being around the people who were willing to remove his normal comfort zone were willing to partake in a journey of personal growth together before his own wings could be flapped—so that he can then soar into the sky and rain down upon the people who need what he learned.

He wants to be a part of that tipping point where the leaf has turned over to obtain abundant life, breathing in new air; taking in new energy.

Monty sought out Logan as an advisor; a companion; and most of all, a friend. Though Monty is not a sheep to the staff held by Dr. Logan Powell, there is major thirst for spiritual knowledge. It then segued into connectivity that required no password. Dr. Logan Powell raises his head and notices men and women being of service to future generations, being arrays of light to the would-be abyss. Logan thinks, *Love conquers hate.*

There is prayer echoing amongst the area; in several languages: English, Spanish, Italian, Arabic, French, German, and Russian. Prayers evocatively sound, even Ray Charles could see that God is present in and around His people.

Dr. Logan Powell, in awe, is grounded from the invigoration which displayed before his very eyes causing humility.

Exuberant, his mind is running one million miles per minute. Logan once envisioned prosperity amongst everyone, even ones who may have been bitter. Faith had succumb to the core of Logan's train of thought that seeds have been sewn—and those seeds shall be manifested for the long hall of each human being there as ripe fruit.

Dr. Logan Powell then turns to Monty, finally asking him, "What's your decision in this whole process?"

Before their invocation, Monty speaking with confidence says, "I have decided to train." They both look each other in the eye—man to man. Monty is of certainty. He nods his head indicating there was no skip in his heart beat—he is ready.

Dr. Logan Powell analyzes Monty's body language; he speaks with his posture straight, and his chest aligned with the heavens,

"I'm proud of you, Monty," says Logan after witnessing Monty's confidence. "This decision is only the beginning for you, and I say that with confidence."

"I notice a glow, similar to Goku's, when he turned to his third level Super Saiyan form," continues Logan, relating to Monty's obsession with Dragon Ball Z's animated story. Monty's jaw dropped; it was then he realized that Logan is not only a mentor, but a true friend.

"Did you watch Dragon Ball Z, as well?!" Monty asks in excitement.

Logan replies, "It was my absolute favorite show as a kid and still is on this very day," smiling at Monty in a friendly manner. "But I hadn't had much time to warp into memory lane."

The connection grows stronger, forming an unbreakable bond of brass links held as tight as a covalent bond. The energy consists of the same high frequency in correlation with each other every step of the way, even if different decisions on destinations were made.

"So are you going to share your decision with me?" Monty candidly asks. "Or am I going to be left in the dark."

"Leaving you in the dark is not possible," replies Logan. "Someway, somehow there will be a spec of light that will be charged into a burst of brightness."

"Alright," playfully says Monty. "Enough already. You're going to make me cry."

Dr. Logan Powell has full respect for Monty. Logan as a teacher and Monty respects his student who has learned quickly under supervision. Logan then shared his decision and says,

"I will be preserving my DNA and one hundred percent of my atoms for future landing." Logan, too, is firm on his decision and bestows his true initial thought.

Logan Powell, ever since his studious times, has learned that the initial thought when making any decision is not to dwell on. Going with his initial thought has lead him to be a man of liberation—the man he is today.

"Do you know what year you would like to return back to life, Logan?" Monty asks, in hope to witness Logan present and well.

"Don't worry, bro. I'll be with you always," Logan says, noticing Monty's regard toward the decision Logan has taken. "If not tangibly, then in spirit," says Logan while patting Monty on the back.

They both embrace each other with a tight hug. Monty regains his composure and they part ways temporarily to go on separate lines before they come face to face with their enrollment kiosk.

As bizarre as it may seem to Logan and Monty, each lined filled with people is conversing of their future plans and bestowing their aspirations on building a civilization and living off of the land. Though stamina will require to prosper on the soon-to-be homeland, people have their mind set-in-stone with the future, unconsciously losing grip of the present moment.

The Law of Attraction is evident in the essence of the people—they put their mind to their decision and made it stick, with the continuity of confidence. Whichever thought has been processed in a timely manner will not be creased, nor will it be folded—it's fresh in their mind; as ripe as they move forward.

They embrace the deliverance to start over and to then forecast their journey into orbit. Teams of architects who have networked and teams of astronauts who have formed, are to facilitate humanity's reach to the stars and beyond.

. . .

For the first voyage, there are two rockets being controlled from Earth to blast into the night sky making their way to the Expanded International Space Station, which supplies food, fuel and other essentials for human progression will be there as storage.

In the outside world, Russia has joins forces with the United States to expand the ISS into an astronomical size—one that can be seen if standing upon the Great Pyramid of Giza during a clear-night sky.

The Cold War between the two nations had grown old and tired out. In a world of trade wars and capitalism, there is room for unity amongst nations, so manuscripts from the illustrious engineer Wernher von Braun, facilitates the technological advances displayed by nations contributing to the intergalactic change to-come.

Wernher von Braun constructed missiles for many countries, many of which included atomic bombs that displayed their overt damage during the world wars which occurred in the early twentieth century. Colonization on another planet such as Mars has been adapted into large scale based on demand and willingness to explore humanity's outreach.

Such manuscripts embody architectural demands which include inspirations deriving from the Italian artist Leonardo Da Vinci. As precise as the drawings and outlines are, they lay the foundation for blueprints to a new future for humanitarian rocketry.

CHAPTER FIVE

There are two sets of training for each task signed up for, whether to be pioneers on Mars' soil or to arrive at a date desired, contingent upon one's credit and down payment. Trainings of movement or non-movement, but nonetheless: training. Training to have the organic aptitude to live on another planet will be detrimental to human survival in the near future.

The corporal private that the commander sent down to the population of people is assisting individuals find their right place which is best fitting with their personal beliefs. Oblivious and totally unaware of the small circles formed within the facility, he learns that with each other he comes into contact with, a firm decision has already been made on their placement

Dr. Logan Powell notices the lack of certainty that formed within the soldier's body language. Logan closes his eyes and wishes him well, for he is confused about his placement adjacent to groups of people that are metaphorically holding arms in faith.

Logan, standing in line, notices the soldier approach him nervously. Dr. Logan Powell looks toward the soldier and rhetorically asks, "Aren't you of all people supposed to have your posture straightened?" Logan scoffs and looks ahead of him. He looks forward to his destination.

The soldier fixes the slouch he approached Logan with and rebutted in anger, "Keep yourself in line." The young soldier is upset with his own self; he could not determine the weakness he had inside of him.

The young soldier is roaming the area and surveying the field. Logan calls him over for a short conversation until he reaches the kiosk.

"Young man, I'm curious, what are the current procedures for the line parallel to the one I'm standing on?" Logan, looking the soldier in the eye, is testing his intellect.

The young soldier cordially gestures to Logan with an open palm to the other line and says, "There is a twelve month intense training period for many of the ones who are going to expedite their colonization on Mars. Their training will be rigorously thorough as they will need to do much cardio and weight lifting to facilitate their bone density decreasing." The soldier continues, "It's interesting, their training; they are training to be astronauts while risking their lives for the greater good—it's heroic to terraform at this early of a stage."

Logan appreciates the young man's words of generosity toward the other group and agreed, "I concur."

The soldier faces Logan and says, "Being on this line, you must know what you want, as well."

Logan keeps his responses short with the soldier, as he is unaware of his true motive, "This is true."

As people are exiting the booth, Logan overhears indistinct chatter amongst Military Police and civilians. He does not give his attention to the noise he hears, as there is an MP who deserves to have undivided attention while doing his job. Logan senses that the young man is essentially a customer service representative for the facility.

Making small talk is not Logan's usual forte, but for the time being, he enjoys the short conversation with the soldier.

Logan thinks, *a wise man once said, 'you get as far as the people you talk to for no reason.'* Logan is a man of productivity and time is always of the essence. He realizes that time is his most valued commodity—it can never be refunded.

"I'm sorry," says Logan. "I need to take heed to what I want."

He then reaches the kiosk and closes the curtain behind him. Logan thinks, *similar to a voting booth.* He sits down and picks up the stylist pen provided. The pen is attached to the counter like a pen to a bank's teller window. Logan is focused, mindset on the goal at hand—to help humanity's future. Carefully and diligently, he reads each module's policy like a lawyer. He finds no bumps or bruises before he places the unique signature to his name. Logan's studies helped with his prompt decision making. He is poring over the kiosk taking every second he is given to complete the task at-hand.

Dr. Logan Powell fills out the miscellaneous information and moves on to the module where he will be risking his finances in accordance with life expectancy.

The next module reads, *Please enter your desired date of arrival.* Logan types in April 1st, 2100. The kiosks calculates the costs in one millisecond and it reads, *Your total amount for this mission is $100,000.00. Please enter your bank routing number and account number.* Logan enters his information and receives a receipt for his transaction, which will be placed on his forearm.

He then is given the choice to pick a location on the
red planet. Before him, on the kiosk, there is a 3D module
where he gets to choose where he wants to land on his
desired date. As the 3D module appears, there is a showing
of Mars in a thermal fashion. In between where it is green
and orange is where he would love to be placed. It is also
near the water, so Incase Logan needs to live off the land,
there is a fine resource. As it is unlikely for those colonizing
the land of Mars to head to the Northern Lowlands.

Logan is on the inclination to seek information in
regards to the whereabouts of where the pioneers of the first
journey may land. He thinks, *or are there people already up
there?* Logan looks to the metallic ceiling and wonders; not
about his decision making but about the future on another
planet.

He picks the region named Northern Lowlands,
Arabia Terra. He is given a number that is engraved by the
kiosk. He places his forearm under a laser-like beam and it
scratches the surface of his melanin skin. It writes, *001215.*
The kiosk then reads, *Thank you very much for your
participation…* and without Logan noticing, his blood
pumping with major adrenaline because of excitement, does
not notice that the kiosk continued its automated transaction
following a fine print, providing further steps on how to

properly prepare for possible life-threatening environmental issues on the embarked celestial body.

Logan is finished with the kiosk and is in a narrow tunnel to reach his goal. He sees the light at the end but understands he will need to be mentally and physically ready for what is set to come: his destiny.

With confidence, Logan pushes the black suede curtain to the side and gazes at the next person—he gestures for them to go ahead inside with no fear. He points to the red leather seat with an open palm and holds the curtain out for them.

"Thank you," says the stranger.

Logan replies, "Godspeed, my friend."

They both smile. Logan walks away from the booth where he then sees Commander Davis fifty feet away, near the fruit stand.

The corporal private abruptly approaches Logan with a clipboard. "And we meet again," says Logan with his arms crossed.

"Yes, it's me, I have one question for you—it shouldn't take too much of your time," responds the soldier.

"Spit it out, son," Logan says to the soldier who is holding minuscule chewing tobacco in his mouth.

The soldier stares up at Dr. Logan Powell, and smirks, "Funny guy, you are." He continues and requests, "Please summarize to me the fundamental steps to your journey"

Logan, with his hands behind his back, responds respectfully, "Well, to my understanding, Contingent upon payment rendered, one may cryogenically freeze themselves into a future date they so desire. In that case me," says Logan as he places his right hand over his chest. Again, Logan, places both hands behind his back with a straight posture and continues his summarization:

"I will stay in a Plexiglas chamber filled with water which would then turn into ice in a matter of seconds for the preservation process to go underway. The chamber's temperature will be recorded at negative four hundred degrees Celsius.

Hence, the participant, being myself"—as Logan leans forward with his abdominal area, speaks clearly and swiftly, "would sustain all the energy needed to live on the red planet itself."

"Okay," says the soldier. "Thank you."

"My pleasure," responds Logan, with a genuine smile.

Logan Powell wants to focus his mind on other matters regarding his perpetual training for the preservation of his atoms, but there was one more request from the soldier: "Sign here, please."

"Sure thing," says Logan as he then signs his name in cursive. Dr. Logan Powell felt a major connection with his inner artistry as he thinks to himself, *Hmm, interesting how writing is, too, a form of art.*

Not only were the words on paper nicely written, the content and substance behind it all backed up its eloquent exterior. Logan thinks, *as long as one has passion for what he or she does and it has a story, why not just throw it in the art pool?*

There is a strong resonance with solving a problem productively. Logan thinks, *many of us have these unsolved*

*equations and within due time and experience, the missing
number in X will find its way.*

Logan reverts back to himself—factors are in-place;
he will keep trotting the upheaval and move forward with
dignity, courage and common sense to help the greater good
of humanitarian psychosis. Logan plans to give individuals
console and peace of mind with organic holistic and spiritual
health, as he specializes in the mind, body, and soul.

With a new environment coming his way, Logan
looks forward to change; *change is inevitable* to Dr. Logan
Powell—it is taken head-on.

For Logan, preparing mentally and physically is
imperative, as he is constantly keen on fruitful nature of a
foundation that cannot be hindered or blemished. He thinks
back to one of his favorite books: The Art of War by Sun
Tzu, as it emphasizes preparation in respect to bloody
battles, but for what it's worth, Logan Powell renders such
tactics as an analogy to his skill set.

For much of that foundation relies on his courage
and resilience, he moves forward in the midst of time
accordingly.

After much meditation, he then perseveres through his thoughts of heavy burden to weigh him down in the very least of his imagination. Logan thinks, *No one is perfect—it matters how we jump the hurdle; it makes us whole. As I jump my hurdle, I will overcome a hill of adversities to see my home on the other side of the bank.*

With the burden being lifted off his shoulders due to his mindset, Logan is present with his chest out and head lifted high. Justification flowed through his mind, and so he thinks out loud while standing alone: "I am going to be on Mars—it is a blessing. This is a chance to reach humanity's star-gazing hump, and I, along with everyone here will be a part of this wondrous process!"

Being in the moment of his own thoughts, Logan is unaware of Monty's presence. Monty, finished with his on-boarding process, approaches Logan with his head up high, confident.

"I can't believe I made this decision to help colonize; to make history!" Monty yelps in excitement.

"That makes two of us, my friend," Logan responds, aware of Monty's changed attitude. He now sees the faith inside Monty and is confident that Monty is making the best decision for himself.

Monty is a young engineer; he has taken steps in his life that will excel his personal and professional development tenfold. "You are worthy of this journey, and I commend you, sir."

"Wow..." says Monty before briefly pausing. "That means a lot, Logan. Thank you."

Monty and Logan walked over to the fruit stand together for the last time before both part ways. While doing so, an intriguing subject conjugates Logan's mind, and he cannot help himself but ask, "Where are you landing, Monty? You know, for the colonization? Where is it all starting?"

"The Northern Lowlands," Monty answers sharply. "That's all I'm able to disclose."

There are eyes and ears everywhere. Military Police are following up with the rest of the population, and there are cameras set up to detect any movements that may seem out of the ordinary from the MP and Commander's perspective.

Although there is cordiality from each soldier, it is sensed by Dr. Logan Powell as a disguise to their main goal:

to obtain as necessary intelligence and data to build up a story in one's personal file.

It is politics; there is a condescending nature to each employee under Commander Davis. Logan is not fond of such environment but does not rebel—he does not see any point in rebelling against a regime who are also trained to kill.

To keep his mind ajar of optimistic opportunities, Dr. Logan Powell thinks while nonchalantly walking with Monty, *I have great confidence in people already being up there. The location I chose in the Northern Lowlands is a popular area. Maybe industrial work up there is booming.*

Monty asks, "Everything ok, Doc?"

Logan chuckles and says, "This is the first time you referred to me as 'Doc.' He proceeds to ask and changes the subject, "Everything ok with you?"

Monty responds, "Yeah, I'm good."

"Good, because so am I," says Logan. "I am in high anticipation for this journey of ours. The feeling will be of ecstasy."

"Agreed," concurs Monty.

Logan and Monty are eating fruit for the final time together before they both go their separate ways—to different training regimens. Logan is eating a vivid green Granny Smith apple and his counterpart is eating a banana.

Without dialogue, their body language disposes of a comfort level perceivably manifesting a clear head and moment seizing.

Logan thinks while chewing on his apple, *I can't believe there will be a civilization there on Mars before I get there. I will see to it that my family is aware of my Destiny's fulfillment—*

Monty breaks the silence and Logan's thinking, "So, your family alright?"

Logan shifts his eyes toward Monty without turning his head and responds, "Yeah, I have faith they're good." Logan continued to open up to Monty, "My kids probably got told some lie by their mom saying 'Your daddy went to go save the world.' Monty, how can I save the world when I can only try to save people? It is up to us to sew a seed of knowledge which in good faith, will turn out to be substantial."

Logan continues to speak, "There's a lot that goes into the fountain of youth. All we can try to do as a village is preserve it with purification, in all regards. That, my friend, will start a tipping point amongst others, to do better." Dr. Logan Powell is speaking with Monty as a friend and speaking in confidence. Monty is listening and mentally note taking the exemplary leadership bestowed by Dr. Logan Powell. "I don't have any clue of what is going on at my home, nor do I have a hint of what my kids are thinking. Yet alone, my wife."

Monty, focuses on what Logan had to say, was caressing his chin and hummed in relation to his understanding, "Hmm."

"Sometimes," Logan says. "I wish my wife would not be with the kids alone. She can be over-aggressive at times...it is sometimes disgusting, but she is the mother of my kids." Logan shrugs his shoulders, "so what can I do, right? — It is all out of my control."

Monty, careful with his words, realizes that this conversation is an open book and responds, "You may be right, Logan, but be careful what you wish for."

"Man, I wish for my kids to be with me in the future on the planet Mars," Logan says, unaware that Dr. Susie Campbell is also listening and watching his every move.

Logan is certain of his words and does not take them back. Affirmatively, Dr. Logan Powell spoke with Monty— Monty notices veins popping out from his forehead.

Monty thought to himself, *This must be Logan's escape.*

It is almost time for both training courses to begin, and Monty was saddened of the bittersweet moment, realizing that Dr. Logan Powell would not be near him through the preserving process.

"You have been like a father to me, Logan," Monty says, looking the man in the eyes, grabbing one of his shoulders.

Dr. Logan Powell then pulls Monty toward his chest and hugs him tightly. "Thank you," they both say simultaneously.

"It's been a pleasure, my dude," says Logan. "Knock 'em dead." Dr. Logan Powell puts his fist up and then thumps his chest with admiration.

CHAPTER SIX

Logan and many others standing before the instructing Drill-Sergeant, are in an element of readiness for the future. The instructor's name is Drill-Sergeant Asia.

Upon giving duties for help on endurance and stamina, everyone preserving their DNA shall serve their bodies well with a plant-based diet. This reminded Logan of a time when he had given a plant-based diet to one of his clients—he was contradicting the institutionalized development for doctors. Holistically and spiritually, with the Law of Attraction as his main ingredient, he helped heal this man of a deathly disease.

Opposing the pharmaceutical field, which distributed medicine Dr. Logan Powell was never fond of, he rebelled against such industry—his kids never received flu-shots. He believes it to weaken the immune system—he believes that it is a contradiction—a hypocrisy in it of itself.

He supplied a number of patients with his non-supplemental nutritional diet, along with routines to follow based on two systems of thinking; simply, System One and

System Two, per Daniel Kahneman's book, *Thinking, Fast and Slow*, one of Logan's all-time favorite reads.

Dr. Logan Powell tracked their process, but he was not reaching his quota for prescribed medicine.

Logan boasted his knowledge for the mind, body, and soul because a scenic route was taken—for the greater good—so that humanity can flourish in its most profound ways, instead of being controlled by medicine that would ultimately make the world a worse place to live in.

. . .

"Alright now, ladies and gentlemen," the Drill Sergeant announces. "Here is your regimen and routine, so stick to it until you all are essentially frozen."

Logan says within himself, a sort of murmur, "Piece of cake." A stranger beside Logan scoffs at his confidence and sought it out as temerity. Logan is not responsive; he ignores the person's ignorance. Logan thought, *The best reaction is no reaction,* and he stands up straight reassuring the stranger he is not one to be hindered of mediocrity.

Logan has his mind set out on a more positive note: throughout each training exercise, Logan aspires to encourage his peers land emphasis on the fact of perseverance; perseverance through anything that may come their way.

Logan is no preacher by licensure, but he indeed knows where his heart lies—and that was within Jesus, his messiah. He manifests the famous bible verse - Philippians 4:13 through clear, vivid tongue: "I can do all things in God that strengthens me."

Logan encourages the people around him say this as a group; not religiously—but spiritually. They all are working in unison. Each drill, day-by-day there is resilience to reach the next level; to reach the top with the guidance of each other.

Logan relinquishes his thoughts and says, "Each one, teach one. Don't just aspire to make a living. Aspire to make a different."

"Hey, Denzel Washington said that!" shouts someone in the crowd.

"Thank you!" replies Logan to the estranged

Some of the group did not believe in Christianity, the Bible or Jesus. But they all were still monotheistic and had begun to give belief in Logan as a prophet of love. Shouting out, Logan speaks, "Love is derived from God. I am a facilitator to lay a foundation of His great blessings upon this voyage." Logan pauses for five seconds, reeling in the attention and continues, "And so are all of you."

With inclusion and positivity, Dr. Logan Powell sheds light upon the dark and exposes inner light within the majority for illumination during one's path in life.

Without regard to everyone's participation on positioning themselves in a positive pivot, there is one segment in the group who perceives themselves as the non-confiding. Logan surveys the area like a comb to hair follicles and senses the energy that is pushing against the prevailing tide.

The rebellion is nonetheless appreciated—it is to not weigh me down, he thought to himself. As he paces back and forth, with hands behind his back, Dr. Logan Powell thought to himself a tad bit longer; and the more he starts to realize that what he is in the wake of something marvelous, a higher inclination on a tipping point begins to arise.

He then calls out the rebellious group and there is a cordial welcome. "What would Jesus do?" Logan asks himself. Dr. Logan Powell continues about his way to speak aloud to the rebellious group in an attempt to show wisdom and to prevent segregation. "Truly I tell you, my people that coming together and joining as one group of energy creates more volume; hence produces more fruit."

Dr. Logan Powell stands on an altar-like platform and he calls them up-front before the rest of the group. The men and women standing at the altar were not polytheistic, but they have no beliefs on a higher power, besides what seems to be their leader: Logan.

"Thank you for coming forward, my brothers and sisters," gratuitously says Logan.

Logan, with a huge task on his open palm is to sew the ripest seed he could into the rebellion nature. After giving all of those men sincere looks, he asked a question which was a catalyst to the long-run activities from these young gentlemen: "What is your calling in life?"

In response, there is none verbal; only body language in which depicted the young men and women to look at each other with confusion. Some shrugging their shoulders, some bowing their heads in embarrassment to never being encompassed and guided on life's journey.

"I am glad you all are confused, even in the slightest at the moment," Logan says, as snickers and murmurs follow from the crowd.

The young men and women had never heard anyone before their very eyes speak with great humility. Many have come from communities that do not seek spiritual guidance as much they seek guidance to monetary gain.

Logan was almost always a facilitator; whether it was of goods and/or services, he was the man to see. Some people depict Logan as their shepherd. And with that title he unknowingly conceived, it sparked the people around him to be of envious nature, which motivated him thus more.

"Listen, my brothers and sisters," Logan says abruptly, cutting off the connecting murmurs like a hacksaw to a tree branch. "I am not sure how to entail it in your brains, but I am going to try...since I clearly noticed that your purposes in life are oblivious to embed with your souls. Each and every single one of you has a purpose in life, whether it may be from teaching kids how to read to help building rockets that will fly us into different galaxies," Logan announces surveying the area, pausing. "I have a testimony and I would like to share it. There was a time during my early twenties, years that I was considered to be insignificant and unworthy on Earth or in the universe."

Everyone, including the Sergeant, starts to lean forward, tuning in to what Dr. Logan Powell needs to say. Not only is he speaking to the young men and women at the altar, but Logan is very much in-tuned to the rabble he helped form. With adrenaline pumping and nerves in a whirlwind, words flowed out like water from a spout.

"I owed it to myself, my family, and those around me to not let anyone feel disappointed knowing that they knew of my talent, my genius-level talent," Logan says, but not in a braggadocio or pompous manner. "And lo-and-behold, I had given much gratitude to this day of being able to speak on encouraging things with my past. I had a prophecy done over me—or foreshadow, if you will, to the calling or purpose in my life. There was a man on an altar, like me, and pulled me out of the masses, hundreds filled the area. I was spoken to by God, and it put my mind at ease.

The man who was a stranger to me, understood me in the most colossal way. I was confused, dwindled—and, so I removed myself from the alter-ego I once displayed. The words this man had spoken of broke me down, as my being was never shattered, but reassembled into the fixed puzzle .

Those words solidified my calling or purpose I have in my life, included with this moment we are all in." So with great enthusiasm, Logan shouted that God will never race us not forsake us. "So if I had gone against his path and disturbed the trust instilled, and still had gotten shown the foreshadow of my future, I know that with will power and determination to fulfill goals is something we can all long for. Thank you, gentlemen...I hope we all learned something."

Dr. Logan Powell, of full-blown humility—trickles a teardrop down his left cheek indicating the utmost appreciation toward life. As he put the first drop to a halt, everyone in the vicinity besides Logan to be in accordance with appreciation. The energy flowing then resonates with each person including the would-be rebels who turned their inner potential into a blooming flower.

Dr. Logan Powell, telling one of his stories and showing empathy for people who may not have known their path to greatness takes in the moment and subsides like a tired man working on a railroad.

Everyone in life has a purpose, thinks Logan. *Whether it may be to endure hardship for the greater good or to use their resources, not limited to the tangible being.*

. . .

With resources that would confide within everyone in the facility, everyone proceeds with their training. *Blood, sweat, and tears* one may call it.

The battle of perseverance swarmed the enemy lines and took the full force of the adventure. Dr. Logan Powell and everyone else involved in the preparation for cryogenically freezing themselves and their DNA, will put their bodies to the test; not everyone will be able to endure the hardship of the negative four hundred degree Celsius freezer.

Not everyone will be able to live when they are released for their desired date, so all of the participants are risk-takers. Contingent upon one's mind, body and soul, willingness to persevere will test the faith of each individual, including Logan.

The Law of Attraction resonates with Dr. Logan Powell, and he makes it his very personal mission to lead by example. To distract himself from the supposed physical hardship being endured, he demonstrates success. He shows the people his fearless tenacity; his courageous persistence; his valorous continuity to help the environment around him.

"Are you a jack of all trades, sir?" says a stranger.

"No, my brother," replies Logan. "I'm just an ordinary man fulfilling a calling."

"I like to go by the following quote: If you don't plan, you plan to fail," says Logan. "Non-fulfillment is not on my agenda. With that, I want to help bequeath the attitude of success among my peers, including you."

"Copy that, sir," says the young man learning from Dr. Logan Powell by analyzing the correlation between actions and words.

"Are you going to sit there and stare or are you going to allow your observation to overtake your actions?" spontaneously asks Logan as he is weightlift training. "Don't let the Sergeant catch you around doing nothing."

"You're right," says the man as he makes his way to train side-by-side Logan attempting to build motivation. "Time to make this a routine."

"That's the spirit," excitingly says Logan.

For breakfast, blended whole wheat grass is on the menu; nothing more, nothing less. For lunch, they indulge on a mixture of beet juice; infused with pineapples and kale. For dinner, they drink water and work out—fasting throughout the night until the next day.

As they become stronger mentally and physically, there is an accord. One accord of resonance that is flowing through the seamless conjuncture which had been presented before them; not by man, but by the ripple of energy which surges through everyone's body. It a unison accord displaying zero forms of hatred. It displays a utopia. An environment where everyone can be themselves, while also treating their bodies as temples making their surroundings a place they can call home.

. . .

Faith conceives throughout the habitat in which the Preservation Group is located. Talks and murmurs of the other group which is training to be astronauts in a very short period of time does not hinder anyone's ability to train thoroughly.

As faith bubbles the circumstances which has been forthcoming to their successful minds, their spiritual nature sparks the other group in the most profound way like a candle helping to light another candle.

Monty, as he is praying before rest, feels a great deal of zest proceed before him. He recollects his thoughts and takes measures into the hands of his own whenever there is any form of unfaithful nature surrounding his temporary abode. Monty, taking after Logan's teaching in good faith, organically learned everything, every gesture, every word spoken, happens for a reason.

Everyone is a teacher in their own way—and it would be a disservice to Monty and to the unfaithful if he is not shedding light upon others that are amongst him or sharing the fruit of which he so ripened.

Monty sees Logan in himself, and that is when he solidifies being a prodigy—a prodigy of moral success; a prodigy of honor.

While Monty prepares to manifest his soul to concerning individuals, the people of the Preservation Group are instructed by scientists of their readiness for the chamber they are going to uphold as their body will immediately freeze.

CHAPTER SEVEN

.Twelve months of routine training pass along, and the moment has come. The moment in which to start a new journey of peace. A new journey to outer space; to reach the stars and moons.

Dr. Susie Campbell abruptly approaches Logan as he is entering the rooms where all the cryogenic chambers are located. "Thank God for technology, huh?" Susie says to Logan as he is looking forward, in amazement with the laboratory and its gadgets.

Logan first takes a short glance of the cylindrical chambers filled with crystal clear water, includes oxygen tubes running along the sides of the base. With ease, Logan turns and responds, "Oh, it's you," as he chuckles. "Are you going to preserve your DNA, as well?"

"Not quite sure about that just yet," says Susie. "Everything must be in order."

"Well, I am sure that is not a problem for you," Logan says in response. "You're a pro," smirking, trying to get a wince of Susie's would-be humor.

She comfortably laughs. Logan notices her sparkly brown eyes, her symmetrically plump smile, which he thinks, *that's the best curve on her body.*

In Logan's eyes, deep down inside, she is his weakness. He could not see past her, just as he could not see past her in his younger years. Logan, thinking of his journey, began to think of reasons why Susie may be standing before him at this very moment. Scrambled in thoughts; blinded by her beauty and wit, he proceeds to not analyze her actions and continues with the moment at-hand.

They both take a walk to Dr. Logan's chamber where he is to spend many years in before being transported over to his desired location on Mars: The Northern Lowlands, Terra Arabia.

Susie asks, with her hands clenched, sweetening the moment with her smile, "So where is the location the magnificent Dr. Logan Powell is heading to?"

Logan responds, "I'm afraid that's classified information, ma'am."

Susie softly replies, "*I promise I will not tell anyone.*" Susie makes a gesture indicating that she will keep quiet. She gestures to zip it, lock it, and then metaphorically toss the key away.

Logan thinks, looks to the ground, *Will she pick that key up?* Dr. Logan Powell stepped back two feet with his hands caressing the curvature of his chin. "If I tell you, will you tell me family?"

Susie responds, stands up straight, "Oh most certainly, captain."

They both laugh at the sarcasm. The engagement between the two sparks a kindle. There is a candle light scorching and no one else in their physical realm could smell or see it—a candle that could only be seen by the beholder of which the flame had come from.

Their gaze speaks of generosity and cordiality. Their gape renders energy which could be felt from any intent to see good in two people interacting. Dr. Logan Powell and Dr. Susie Campbell feel at-ease with each other. There is no uncomforted vibe in their current setting. The slightest bit of dullness is slayed by every bit of invigorating vibrancy.

Suddenly, Logan drifts from this energetic feeling with Susie tuned in to his family, whom are unaware of his location at the moment, nor is he aware of their whereabouts.

"Everything alright, Doc?" asks Susie, suspicious of Logan's focus on her.

Dr. Logan Powell seizes the recollection of his family's welfare and proceeds to think positively—he speaks out loud, "Oh how I cannot wait to see my family, especially my little ones." Logan looks down in sincerity, not hoping for acknowledgement on his caring nature, but hoping that Dr. Susie Campbell, with her clout, would be able to get his family, at least his children, to The Northern Lowlands, Arabia Terra, Mars.

Distraught, Susie holds back her true emotions with a happy facade and says, "And you should see to it, Logan."

Dr. Logan Powell put his right palm on the Plexiglas chamber and prays to himself; bowing his head. As he was praying, he thinks outloud, "Well, I guess this will be my home for many years to come until landing." He could feel the excitement rushing through his body, the adrenaline rush to his brain, and the humility rush to his heart.

Logan looked to his right, over his bicep; his eyes only being visible to Susie, "Do the right thing."

"Sorry?" Susie asked. "I could not hear you, sir."

Logan stood up straight, approached her, holding her by the waist, gazing Susie in her sparkling brown eyes, "Do the right thing; you understand?"

Susie's heart was racing. Her mind running one million miles per minute, she is not able to speak the words she has on her mind, but she does say a couple of words for reassurance: "Will do, Logan." Looking to her right and left, making sure the coast is clear, she kisses Logan on the cheek, making her mark as she landed her lips on the surface of his skin.

Logan looks at his reflection from the glass, with a facial expression of concerning nature.

"Organic lipstick?" Dr. Logan Powell asks, as his curiosity is engulfed with the liabilities of any bacteria being put his chamber.

"Yes, sir," says Susie, and then smiles—knowing why he asked.

Logan got undressed; being physically naked is
necessary for the process of preserving anyone's DNA while
cryogenically frozen before transportation into a new world.
The doctor overseeing his chamber approaches the water-
filled embodiment and asks Logan, "All set, my friend?"

Logan nods in agreement and responds, "All set.
Let's rock." He takes one final look at Susie before he is shot
with a needle that tranquilizes his body into coma.

Logan is carried by a lift by the ankles, wrists and
waist as he is now sound asleep. The lift is made up of straps
and is similar that of a hospital bed, but with a lot less
cushion. It is a bed that is designed like a flexible canoe to fit
the contours of the body perfectly.

The metal frame and rubbery straps hold Logan down
before he is ready to be placed inside the waters. The
overseeing doctor then climbs up to the mechanism and
places an oxygen mask onto Logan.

While this is happening, Dr. Susie Campbell is
amazed by the technology that is proceeding before her. She
is dumbfounded at the astronomical possibilities of
everything under the Sun, as humans are able to be
transported into the future. She is electrified, and she is
thinking about what Logan said to her, not once, but twice:

Do the right thing. He is then dipped into the chamber of freezing cold water smoothly, causing no splash.

Susie closes her eyes for a brief second, nods her head and immediately turns back to the direction of the Commander's post. She is walking, but not with a congruent conscious; her mind is taking on different shapes and forms.

Dr. Susie Campbell snaps out of it and focuses on the matter at-hand: *Do the right thing,* she thought. She wipes away a slew of thoughts running circles in her head when she finally puts them to a halt, as she arrives at Commander Davis' chamber.

"Everyone out," commanded Davis. Soldiers scatter and scramble to find an exit as Dr. Susie Campbell has an announcement to make to Commander Davis. All four soldiers leave in accordance as Susie has her hands together below her waist and lips tightened in a modest state.

Seated on his computer chair behind his mahogany-wooden desk, Commander Davis cordially welcomes Susie to sit across from him. "What is it, Dr. Campbell? How can I help you?"

Susie sits down, loosens her hair, and looks Commander Davis in the eye. She does not hesitate to speak her mind. "I need to leave this facility and head over to California," she says firmly.

"Is that right?" Davis asks.

"Yes, sir," says Susie, with a poker face, not letting Commander Davis look past her motive. She is resisting the gradual nature he endures when sitting behind his desk, as if he is conducting rigorous business.

Susie is sitting up straight, legs crossed and her hands clenched like a royal princess; she is a confident woman performing a task of second-nature ability. Although it may be intimidating and arduous to some surrounding Commander Davis around the clock, Dr. Susie Campbell has the art of persuasion down to a science.

"You know I cannot let you out of these walls, Doctor," says the Commander.

Susie Campbell stands up, with her hands on the desk, staring at Commander Davis directly in the eyes. She envisions her mission as important, so she pushes the envelope and presents her cleavage to Mr. Davis.

With bold confidence in herself, Susie says, "I know you want me, Commander...it is obvious with the way you stare at me...oh and how you want me alone?" Susie scoffs, "Face it, I'm all there is around here...for...you know" as she winks. "I only need two days," says the doctor, as she is aware of her inducement onto the married Commander.

"Two days," says Commander Davis, eradicated.

"In writing please," commands Susie.

As Commander Davis scrambles for paperwork, he says "Your wish is my command." He rapidly writes up a waiver and signs it. "Two days, Susie. Don't make me come hunting for your ass."

"You got it, boss," Susie replies.

• • •

Dr. Susie Campbell makes her way to the exit; she is escorted out of the facility by a corporal private. With a goal in mind, Susie's motive is to locate Dr. Logan Powell's wife and kids.

As she steps out of the facility, she takes a long whiff of fresh air. *Ahh,* Susie exhales in comfort. A black government-issued car is waiting for her.

The driver steps out and hands her a clipboard with a paper on top disclosing her to sign off on the vehicle she is going to operate for forty eight hours total. "If you, the operator are not back within 48 hours, there will be a team of government officials out to detain or terminate you, under their discretion," says the agent.

"Thanks," says Susie. "I just read that." Out of curiosity, she asks, "Which turn is west of the country?"

He looks at her for a brief second with a bland facial expression and points, "That way, ma'am."

CHAPTER EIGHT

Susie enters the vehicle after signing off. Grabbing the wheel and proceeding to turn on the ignition, she is stuck with the precedence of *doing the right thing*.

Susie Campbell drives down the road listening to her favorite song: "One More Time" By Sam Cooke in relation to her past interconnection. Susie passes through the Yerington cutoff and focuses on her way due west.

After an elongated drive of twelve hours, Susie reaches her destination: Logan Powell's home—Los Angeles, California—North Hollywood Hills.

With extended research, Susie reaches the home of Dr. Logan Powell and his family—and approaches the front doorstep of their four-acre homeland surrounded by white-picketed fencing boasting on a hill of which there are many trees nesting the singing birds bringing out the melodies unique in their own substance.

Susie thinks to herself, *Let's make this quick.* Dr. Susie Campbell ambles to her knowledge as Logan's home. She knocks three times and then rings the doorbell afterwards, giving a five second pause between the knock and the ring. Susie hears footsteps approach the door; she gets prepared to speak with Logan's wife, but one of the children answer. "Hello, ma'am—who are you?"

"Hi sweetie," Dr. Susie Campbell responds with a welcoming smile—her teeth as white as snowfall on arctic winters at Yosemite National Park. Susie hunkers down, reaches common and tangible ground with Logan's eleven year old son. "You must be Arnold," she says as she takes a strand of light brown hair into her palm.

"Hey!" Arnold shouts, as he grabs Susie's right-sided wrist. "How do you know my name?" Arnold, age eleven, is intuitively inclined to acquaint with the unknown.

"Why, I'm Susie Campbell," she says, astonished by Arnold's initiative and aptitude for awareness. "Hasn't Logan, your Dad, ever mentioned me?" — Logan's wife appears before Arnold could respond, "May we help you?" asks Sheila Powell.

Susie Campbell, standing on the welcome mat, smiles and greets Sheila. Without asking Logan's wife for her name or before an introduction is had, Susie intersects without a signal—and they crash without dialogue. A ten second stare at each other builds ten minutes worth of rapport to the eyes of each beholder.

Sheila suddenly shuts the door behind her. Arnold, star struck and confused, runs along to tell his older sister, Anna, the news. They both gaze outside the window directly above the white pillars looking over the porch and walkway to the house.

As Sheila recollects her thoughts, witnessing Arnold go upstairs, she silently opens the door to learn of the sudden visit from Dr. Susie Campbell.

Upstairs in the kids' bedroom, with the window having a child safety lock on it, the Arnold and Anna are only able to pore over on the gestures and facial expressions from Susie and their mother.

"Is this really our only way of eavesdropping on their discussion?" softly asks the twelve year old Anna.

"I guess," says Arnold, shrugging his shoulders. What do you think their talking about?"

Anna rebuttals, "Or whom?"

The two siblings both stare at each other with grim and concerning appearances. Anna holds her little brother's hand as they carefully watch the conversation take place below them.

Susie and Sheila shake hands in settlement. Such agreement is not entirely sought out by the kids watching above. They seek further clearance by waiting for their mother to return into the house, while to find them upstairs together, holding hands in the vestibule, seated on the bench adjacent to the Steinway and Sons Piano.

With a yellow envelope filled with signed important, top-secret files, Sheila approaches her children and hugs them both tightly. "Mommy needs to go." With resentment in her tone, she whispers, "I'm trying to do the right thing," with tears of guilt running down her cheeks.

Sheila sinks her chin on two shoulders: Anna's left and Arnold's right. On her two knees, there was no forgiveness to be expressed as Susie looms over, tuning in with her arms crossed.

What's done is done, thinks Susie.

Anna asks, "What's wrong, what's going on?"

"Shhh…" Sheila shushes her daughter with an index finger over the lips she helped bring into Earth.

Before Arnold could speak, Sheila utters in melancholy: "I love you both—please know that."

"We love you, momma," they both respond, as they wipe the chunky cheeks that filled with baby fat and condensation released from their soul onto the skin's surface.

Sheila continues, "I can't explain much right now, so please go with the nice woman downstairs."

Susie, waiting patiently downstairs in front of the two fifteen-foot pillars, which surrounded a red door embodying a brass parabolic-shaped door bell, had her hands behind her back, defenseless as can be.

The kids walk downstairs, afraid of Dr. Susie Campbell, shoulders subside below their heart as they're seated on the velvet-smooth cushion.

"You're going on a trip," says Sheila. "It'll be worth every penny"—Sheila stutters, "I mean, minute. Please cherish each moment with each other."

The children are confused and dumbfounded by the news. Anna and Arnold, scratching their heads, are sent to an abyss of darkness, sunken into a whirlpool of mud in which they do not know how to get out.

"Where will you be, Mom?" Arnold asks, with tears drying up below his eyes; between the bridge of his nose and each eye lay a dried set of tangible emotion from the human body. Human emotion which appears in condensation0like format, requiring feeling and love to take place. Arnold tries his best to transition to a place of neurological solitude. Holding his sister's hand firmly, with the feeling of going downhill 70 degree angle at 80 miles per hour, he tries to make an upheaval into the horizon. Anna reciprocates the grip bestowing her presence in this distorted time for Arnold and the lack of understanding.

"Just know, I will be with you spiritually, always," Sheila says, shifting her eyes to each pair of retinas before her. However the compromise, familial invigoration constantly sticks with Sheila Powell. She caresses their heads full of hair and curiosity.

· · ·

Arnold and Anna Powell walk downstairs, following their mother. There is perplexity in the bearing hailed from the children's gloom-filled energy. Dr. Susie Campbell embraces them with open arms.

The children have no authority to the adults'
decision-making. The oppression from child to adult ignites
resonation with Anna—she remembers a scene in the movie
'Matilda.' In the movie, Matilda's dad expresses the nature
of a frustrated father whose power-trip gets between him and
his children. She closed her eyes and used analogies to better
comprehend the situation at-hand. "I'm big you're small, and
there's nothing you can do about it," Anna recalls in the
hippocampus region of the brain, part of the limbic system.

Both Arnold and Anna, look back, waving at their
mother goodbye. "Bye, Momma!" they both shout-out
simultaneously.

Sheila replies, as she is waving, still with Susie's
delivered envelope in her hand, "It's not goodbye; it's see
you later!"

CHAPTER NINE

While holding the passenger door open for the children, Dr. Susie Campbell also sends a farewell-wave to Sheila, winking at her with a smirk that Sheila does not see. With no bags packed, minds stranded in confusion, Anna and Arnold step foot into the government-issued vehicle and ride back to the mid-western facility.

The children, scared, intuitively boast madness amongst Dr. Susie Campbell—she could see their facial expressions from the rear-view, and so she adapted. "Hey, kids, how about some music?"

The children turn their heads toward one another and nod in agreement to make this unknown ride a long one. "Let's listen to hip hop," Anna says, smiling. "Any artists come to mind, Susie?"

Holding the steering wheel with both hands, Susie carefully examines the road ahead of her. In her line of vision, she is looking toward the horizon, waiting for her destination to-be. "Sorry, Anna?" She startles and replies. "I was daydreaming."

"Never mind," says Anna, rolling her eyes. She playfully hits Arnold on the bicep in unison to Susie turning on the radio tuning in to music. She finds nothing of interest and starts to hum a melody she deems beautiful.

Susie, with the sound from her vocal cords, composes a hypnotizing-like rhythm sending the children into a deep sleep. Susie's vocals spark a sound wave into the essence of the vehicle which then soothes the air into a lavender-scented mood aligning with the air-freshener attached to the car's air conditioning vent.

• • •

Several hours later, Susie Campbell, Anna and Arnold arrive at the facility. Awaiting in front of the steel doors that lead to an underground facility are three government agents, one of which who handed the keys to Dr. Susie Campbell.

In a way of being as discreet as possible, no words were spoken, but nodding of the head from each person in confirmation while Susie was still in the driver's seat is exchanged.

As the kids were still sound asleep, the government agents carefully placed blindfolds over their already-closed eyelids before allowing entrance into the facility

Arnold wakes up and is startled—opening his eyes not being able to see, the feeling of fright seizes him. Famished, he cries aloud, "What's going on?!" He attempts to remove the blindfold but he is restricted with sound wave sterilization. He nor Anna are quite sure what is being endured. Their melancholy causes Susie to act fast; to nurture them into a tranquilization. Susie Campbell has no children of her own, but has the knowledge and aptitude to be a nurturing mother.

"No worries, little children," says Susie playing the motherly role with a soothing tone of voice. "I'm here, and I have a delightful treat ahead for you two."

Anna and Arnold grow assuagement with Susie Campbell. Rapport builds from the ground-up, and it is Dr. Susie Campbell's personal objective to make sure the mental stability for Logan's children are of a sane equilibrium.

Dr. Susie Campbell makes sure of no shortages or surpluses; spreading herself thin or wide was not an option— being pinpoint to the bullseye is her accuracy for mental alignment. Doctor and mother-like instincts helps create a homeostasis she so dubs as general knowledge for human care.

Anna and Arnold, the only kids in the facility, and amazed at the state-of-the-art equipment, they are oblivious to their environment. Anna kindly asks, "Where are we, Susie?"

"Think of this place as Disney Land, Anna," responds Susie, keeping the truth from the child.

As soon as she has steps foot in the building, there are eyes and ears on every square foot. Commander's chambers pay close attention to each motion made, whether done silently or with sound. Like a casino's security team, they have IBM-like technology keeping track of each gesture, autonomously taking notes on any patterns.

Without the awareness of Anna and Arnold, Susie Campbell instinctively escorts the young boy and girl to the chambers in command. Commander Davis, with his arms crossed, waiting at the one-way mirror sliding doors surrounded by steel framing, greets Susie and the children. "Oh what a pleasure it is to have you two at the facility," Commander Davis says. "I've heard wonderful things." Anna and Arnold, holding hands, stare at each other, catch on to the condescending attitude bestowed by the Commander.

"Hello," says Anna, taking initiative to speak to the Commander without getting introduced by Susie. "I'm Anna and this is Arnold, my brother."

Commander Davis makes eye contact with Dr. Susie Campbell, making a mental note on her lack of manners being perceived assuming her will to introduce the children.

"Well it is lovely to meet you two," Commander replies. "I am Commander Davis, and you are in my chambers, where the magic happens," says Davis as he shifts the peripherals of his hazel brown eyes toward Susie as she confides. "You kids like magic, don't you? - Every kid loves magic."

"Can you make our father appear within the next two minutes?" Arnold bravely asks the Commander.

Susie Campbell puts her head down in shame. In a tone of resentment, she says, "Yeah, can you?"

"Oh yes, I can," replies the Commander confidently with his back straightened, hands at his rear. "Let's go."

"Yes ..." says Anna, blandly enthused. "Let's."

Arnold looks at his watch, sets a timer, keeping the Commander honest in relation to such magic tricks being performed in a timely manner. As the door slides open with the motion of four bodies walking toward it, Arnold starts the timer at two minutes, and stares at the Commander and Dr. Susie Campbell, his colleague.

Speed walking, the Commander is keeping himself at honesty for entrustment from the children of Dr. Logan Powell. The rest of the group follows suit and keeps up with the Commander as he rushes through each door, scanning his keycard for security clearance.

With anticipation on the upheaval, Anna and Arnold's eyes start to widen with excitement, for they have not come across the physical presence of their father in several months. Anna, the older sibling, becomes in awe. Her eyes glisten in amazement, as she is holding her brother's hand tighter by the second, disregarding the two-minute promissory duration.

Arnold gradually checks his digitized watch, and suddenly looks up intending to comment on the timing. "Okay—here we are," says Commander Davis with an open palm, welcoming everyone, including Dr. Susie Campbell, who then analyzes the children's reactions to seeing their father in the flesh.

Both Anna and Arnold release their physical bond and their sensation is not mutually exclusive. The frequencies of their energy are in correlation on the same plain.

They are in a feeling of apprehension. Appreciative of the heroic efforts displayed by their father to take on a new planet by force, Anna and Arnold simultaneously develop into teary human beings with precipitation of happiness and hope subsiding from their soft cheeks. They both approach the Antarctic cylindrical glass and seamlessly touch it with an open palm connecting with the naked body inside the glass to be their blood relative, their father, the exhilarating substance with eyelids shut.

Anna and Arnold both placed their torsos on the glass, attempting to hug their father—Dr. Logan Powell. Attempting to do so, the tip of the outstretched hands softly collides with one another. The columnar isof a large circumference and large enough to surpass their other set of fingers touching each other's.

With observation from Commander Davis and Dr. Susie Campbell, opportunity strikes. In respect, Commander Davis becomes sentimental to the gesture displayed by the children; sincerity and consideration fills his soul. Commander Davis takes a step back into an abyss and bows his head. The light which is illuminated in the room was conducted by the children's love for their father.

Enlightened, Dr. Susie Campbell approaches the children, smiling, also appreciating their body language which then creates a tipping point of affection unto her. She circles the barrel-shaped glass—and as she does so, Susie descends to one knee, and then to the other, subsequently into tangible common grounds with Anna and Arnold.

The ethereal commonalities she presents take place when both her hands came into formality with the children's finger tips as a circular trifecta. Tangibly, then outlines a circle of trust around the thick and cold glass Logan is hibernating in, formed by the curvature of their arms interconnecting. Moments later, they all release their cheeks from the ice-cold glass. With blood reaction being dynamic, their one side of each face from the trifecta was blushed.

Between the interim times of cold-temperature toleration, each part of the circles remembers a moment with Logan. Their imaginative presence into the past creates a jolt of energy sparking the nature of the ensued environment.

Anna reminisces the moment of her familial adventure that includes her father being a guide during their vacation in New York City. Anna envisions many people amongst her while spending time in the Big Apple. She was a worm of knowledge that sprung across the massive grid of Manhattan.

Anna enjoyed the history her father had known and was a sponge to the lectures of all subjects spoken of. She was most intrigued by the New York Public Library and adjacent to it, is Bryant Park where she and her family once had a picnic on the perfectly maintained lawn.

Both landmarks were enriched with history that followed a foundation of historical events taking place. She appreciated the Stephen A. Schwarzman building and considered it a temporary sanctuary.

Nothing lasts forever, she constantly thought.

Throughout the three-week stay at The Edition Times Square, she would visit the temple of books and manifest her discoveries and share what she learned with Logan, Sheila and Arnold. It then excelled her personal development, allowing her to speak her feelings in eloquent fashion.

She gained knowledge through books and maps, involving herself in the afflictions of scientology and different perspectives of the world, whether geographical or religious. Her parents, Logan and Sheila Powell, are role models, as they are to Arnold.

Arnold transformed hugging of the cylindrical stud with conceptualizing his tangible being with his father's. Dr. Logan Powell, with help from Sheila, led by example among their sprouts.

Specifically, Arnold generated knowledge from his father as a very young child, challenging teachers in the elementary classroom when his intuitive nature would strike the rebellious contours of his environment.

Arnold gained knowledge from the outside world, along with knowledge from his home. Frequently, Arnold would consider himself a young man, a cub to a king of the jungle, he thought of his father—a leader. Arnold had the privilege of learning to flap his wings whenever educated on a valuable life lesson he would receive not only from Logan, but from Sheila, as well.

Overwhelmed with the worrisome nature of his mom, Arnold was geared to be around his Dad—to take after him as an example to the world in which he is in. Sought out to be like his father, mental notes from Arnold would be embedded for future references; with every story or action, came a reason to be in the midst.

Arnold honored his parents, as they fill mind of both he and his sibling with nature-infused antics, like Voltaire's belief in deity.

Commending the great nature bestowed before them, they realized that stars align correctly with organic compounds and appreciation. Indebted energy had become the foregrounds and cornerstone for a diamond-like foundation during the childhood. The colossal-like idea manifested into being grounded; down-to-earth like gravity.

With Arnold amongst his peers, he would stand out; remembering a time where male peers of his were insulting another person. With morals laid upon thee, Arnold refers back to a time where his dad provided education within the subject of loving oneself.

During the insulting encounter, he candidly asked his peer, "Do you love yourself?"

Stammered, reluctant and stunned, there was a lag in the boy's answer. He disconnected from the current being and had become uncomfortable with no verbal exchange to be had.

Arnold took a mental note, and continued to challenge, "One should not say anything bad about another human being; no one's life is better than another's." Arnold paused for a moment, eyes focused on his aura while his lips were moving swiftly when speaking. "My father taught me that; maybe we can all learn from grown-ups, after all," Arnold continued to speak emphatically.

Exceptional was the proposition from Logan and Sheila's son; throughout everyday life, there was an agenda to follow, whether it may change or be of stagnation in its logistical stigma.

Dr. Susie Campbell, on the other hand, had an agenda of her own. Scattered thinking, Susie's mental capacity scrambles to confide with the spiritual connection she may have had with Logan. Squinting her eyes, she thinks—her mind is pressed against time, she is inclined to memorize a moment of clarity in which occurred with Logan.

During her train of thought, Susie gives strength to the invigorating time spent with Logan during the initial stages of Cryogenic behavior. Amid her time with Dr. Logan Powell, rapport was gained—and she felt a connection; a connection in which had no lag; a connection in which placed her on an inclination to make it her personal goal to be in the midst of Logan Powell's physical frame yet again.

A predisposition is proposed within the mind of Dr. Susie Campbell, and it was the energy-filled journey to be partnered with Dr. Logan Powell.

Nothing is going to chastise the embodiment set forth for my journey, Susie thinks selfishly.

"It's time to go," abruptly says Commander Davis.

With final thoughts being eroded by Anna and Arnold Powell, they departs from their position of entrusted energy with their father after Susie decides to rise on Davis' command. The two siblings say farewell to their Dad.

"Till next time, sir," Arnold says gratuitously, staring back over his shoulder as he is leaving the cryogenic setting with the rest.

"Dad will always be with us, Arny," Anna says, looking her in the eye, caressing his blushed cheek. "I will be with you side by side until we are all reunited in the open space."

Arnold kisses his sister on the cheek and replies, looking toward his feet, "Thank you, Anna."

"Please, kid," she replies chuckling. "Don't show me your thanks. I'm doing my job as family, and especially as an older sister."

"You're only about a year older than me, Anna," says Arnold. "Simmer down."

Commander Davis interjects, "You kids know why Dr. Susie Campbell has brought you to this location, correct?"

"To be shown our dad?" Anna sarcastically replies.

"Not only that," Davis replies. "You will be cryogenically placed alongside your dad for year 2100. You and your younger brother have a bright future ahead." Anna senses no satire from the Davis.

Holding her brother's hand, she looks at him in confinement and asks Commander Davis, "How will the process follow?"

"Dr. Susie Campbell will take care of you and your further questions at this point in time; please follow her, and she will instruct you accordingly," Commander Davis responds. He squats down, gently places his palm on their back, in between their shoulder blades and directs them toward Dr. Susie Campbell who smiles and welcomes them with open arms.

"Come children," Susie says, walking with Anna and Arnold, while then looking over her shoulder at Commander Davis for confirmation.

Commander Davis nods his head in discretion and lifts his right hand forward with a palm to indicate her precedence to cordially walk with the children to their proposed destination.

Anna and Arnold, comfortable, but unaware of their next line of sight, are whimsical of their environment.

"I am excited!" shouts Arnold. "We're going to be just like dad, Anna!"

Anna looks toward her brother while walking down the corridor, smiling, "Yeah, Arny. Just like dad."

Hearts pumping with volatile excitement to see what life has in store during every step on the way through the tube-like hallway, which has outskirts of steel plating.

Anna looks to her left, seeing herself in mirror-like fashion on the German-manufactured and polished steel, flips her hair as she nonchalantly walks through the narrow abyss of silence between she and Susie.

"I still want to know how you know our dad," says Arnold with a stern facial expression. "It doesn't occur to me how fast all of this is happening. Why are *we* getting picked? Is there an ulterior motive behind these actions?"

Susie Campbell reacts—she tightens her grip on Arnold's hand and stops walking and squats down and in a low, serene voice she says, "Hush now, child. Don't worry about a thing, okay?"

Anna is tuning in to the conversation and is also wondering of Susie's intentions but says nothing—just analyzes.

"Everything happens for a reason," Susie says. "Isn't that one of your father's mantras?"

Anna takes a glance at Arnold after Susie quotes their father. She gestures him with her index finger on her lips to keep quiet. "Yes, that is our father's saying," Anna says squinting at Dr. Susie Campbell's backside.

Susie shifts her peripherals toward the direction of the comment made, and she sniffs loudly.

"Hey, share some oxygen for the rest of us," Arnold jokingly says. The children snicker together, and then it becomes laughter.

They invigorated themselves into Dr. Susie Campbell's oblivion—they are living in their own moment; their moment of humanity. Their expansion on humanity's life with the gift of laughter—the gift to be happy, even when faced with a hardship of confusion for their next step and continued agenda is something only to be built from their home environment.

Dr. Susie Campbell stands upright, and then tugs them toward her direction like an angry babysitter tolerating their line of work. The three of them arrive at the screening for evaluation.

"What's next, Susie?" asks Anna.

"Yeah, what's next?" follows up Arnold.

"Are you afraid of needles, kids?" asks Susie.

"Needles schpeedles," says Arnold, not intimidated. "Bring it on already."

"Yeah," agrees Anna. "We can take it."

After the screening, Dr. Campbell gives them both a shot from a needle that will excel their immune system to become strong children; one hundred times stronger than the average child.

"This is a plant-based substance, children," says Susie, holding a clipboard. "How do you feel?

"Sleepy," blandly says Anna. "Is it nap time already?"

"Hahhh," Arnold follows up with a yawn. "Where's my bed?"

Observing, Susie takes note, "Hmm, interesting."

"Kids, this will make you strong and healthy," Susie says in a friendly voice.

The children are calm, waiting on the next step that is going to be performed by Dr. Susie Campbell. Waiting patiently, Anna and Arnold notice the swift nature of the procedure and do not question her abilities to do her job in a calm matter.

With high stakes, Dr. Susie Campbell carefully places the final set needle in each arm, inside the elbow. She does this in simultaneous fashion.

"You're amazing at this," Anna says, complimenting Susie on the operation.

"Just another day in the office," replies Susie, smiling at Anna, without showing her teeth. "All done!" Susie rises off her office chair, which assisted on a straight posture. She grabs the needles which will then tranquilize the children into the deepest sleep they have ever had.

Jotting down notes for record keeping, Dr. Susie Campbell finalizes the experiment and dubs it as a success. She excelled their advancement toward the objective before the main course: cryogenically freezing the two children without providing them necessary training.

Checking their vitals, Susie thinks to herself, *Wow, it actually worked. What a shot in the water.*

"As precise as a fisherman with a harpoon," says Anna, congratulating Susie.

"Agreed, sis," says Arnold, looking over at Dr. Campbell.

Dr. Susie Campbell looks down, afraid of what Dr. Logan Powell may think after she applies the sedatives to his kids' bodies. She snaps out of the pessimistic train of thought, as she is cognizant of the prerequisite in order for them to be tranquilized during the process of the cryogenic preservation.

The excitement displayed by the children is shut down immediately with their bloodstream coming to a halt. With a sedative consumption running along their veins, brain activity is slowed. The children are therefore unable to comprehend what is going on in the present time.

From Anna and Arnold's perspective, Dr. Susie Campbell is seated between both of their medical beds working on them in unison. Her voice transforms into audio player-like fashion.

"By the time you know it, you will be awake in Mars, beside your father, Logan Powell," Dr. Susie Campbell explains, as she knows that unresponsiveness will occur from the children's sterilization.

"He once said that he will never leave, nor forsake his children," she continues to say as the children's eyelids drape gently.

Dr. Susie Campbell instructs her delegation to take heed of the children's bewilderment—and to place them next to their father, Dr. Logan Powell. Shortly thereafter, four assistants arrive and inform Dr. Susie Campbell of their acknowledgement for the request made. Air compressors make a sound, indicating that the door has opened.

"You called for us," the lead assistant says.

Each of them then pick a bed to grab; two to each cot. Carefully, like a pallbearer, they hold the beds above their waist—and hold strongly with firm grip after Dr. Susie Campbell straps them down so that they can be steady.

Feet up on his desk, Commander Davis plays Vivaldi's Four Seasons in his chambers as the delegates stride along the corridor pacing themselves to each melody enlightened. The sound waves ride throughout the environment, illuminating the dark abyss and turmoil from the ulterior motives which have been displayed within the minds of the facility's leaders.

Rushing through the lay of the land, Dr. Susie Campbell races behind the delegations holding the beds of Anna and Arnold. She asks them kindly to place them down, in the event where she decides to kiss them on the forehead.

"See you later," she whispers.

Violins continuing to sound from the surrounding speakers, Dr. Susie Campbell races to the chambers of command. At the peak of the Vivaldi's melody, she storms inside, where Commander Davis is waiting for her, leaned back, hands folded across his chest.

"You know, I have been waiting for you," says the Commander, comfortably seated.

Responding candidly, Susie says, "Oh, is that right?"

Commander Davis sits up, and places his hands which are still folded, on the desk and leans forward, "Yes that is right." With his right index finger, he then calls for her. Dr. Susie Campbell is hesitant, but the Commander does not make a mental note as he is blinded by the hopeful future.

"You know, I'm not your pet," says the smiling Susie. With the upper hand engraved in her mind, she calmly walks over to Commander Davis. He is ready and willing, but unsure if he is able to take control.

Susie analyzes and sits down across from him, as if she is going to negotiate. Crossing her legs and hands, Susie does not distort the matter. She leans forward showing her cleavage and pulls Commander Davis' head forward to her breast, and he succumbs to her nature of lust.

He tugs on her hair, letting his mind run amuck, while then forcing his physical frame over the table to become one with Susie. Susie contributes, and with an ulterior motive in mind, she makes his time worthwhile.

Commander Davis' ring-wearing left hand is exposed to his vision as he runs his fingers along the body of Dr. Susie Campbell's. With lustful eyes, they both impart into the vision of one another, both having different motives within their actions. With clothes coming off, both enter into a depth which they will not be able to climb out of.

A hole very deep, there will need to be assistance for restitution. With border-line conscience on Commander Davis' mind, he enters Susie Campbell with no regret. With each stroke, he gives in to the embodiment of his wife and is internally naked.

Stripped and cold blooded, Commander Davis releases Susie, as he then comes into thought. Suddenly, he realizes the love he has for his wife and internally asks for forgiveness to the higher power of himself.

Hmm, perfect timing, thinks Susie.

Dr. Susie analyzes the vulnerable state and requests enter the Mars capsule that has been left behind for emergency purposes by pointing in the direction of the "Emergencies Only" sign.

With guilt and blackmail in mind, Commander Davis grants Dr. Susie Campbell the request, as he regains his composure. Susie puts down her dress and repairs herself into a calm state of mind.

Dr. Susie Campbell gently grabs Commander Davis' chin and informs him, "Nothing happened." Susie, with her confident strut, then turns around, "Do the right thing."

Commander Davis, with his pants off, finds himself in a state of regret. With his head down, he nods his head and gestures for Dr. Susie Campbell to go away. Susie also nods her head in a bodily gesture to grant Commander Davis his space for rest and recuperation.

CHAPTER TEN

Dr. Susie Campbell walks out of the commanding chambers and through the sliding doors with more confident than ever before. She pauses and smiles—galvanized because she now possesses the opportunity to make her way to the bases of Mars whenever at her leisure. Her opportune moment is taking place before her, as Susie walks toward the kiosk where the capsule awaits her to be seated.

As she approaches, the kiosk senses movement and robotically sounds, "Please provide the authorization number and state your name."

With no hesitance, Susie Campbell provides the robot with answers. "I am Dr. Susie Campbell, A.I. Number One Six Nine, and I have been granted access from Commander Davis. Please confirm."

"Confirmed," sounds the kiosk. The kiosk then provides instructions and requests for Susie to choose her destination.

"Northern Lowlands, Arabia Terra" she decides firmly. Susie walks into the capsule and prepares for liftoff.

VORTEX

Dr. Logan Powell, frozen, is in a state of mind where he is dreaming. He is deep dreaming into his past from his most climatically points to the falling resolution which then fluctuates more than a currency valuation chart. Logan had grown up in the city of New York, the Bronx. He and his parents stayed near the Yankees stadium, "The house that Ruth built." Logan and his dad were enlightened into the sport of baseball—it was his father's dream to become a right-fielder in the Major Leagues, and it did not matter what team he played with, for as long as he had gotten a chance to touch the same grass as George Herman Ruth, Jr.

Logan's dad, Henry Powell, idolized "Babe" Ruth. There was not a moment in time while playing catch Henry did not revere after Mr. Ruth. "He was the Yankees best slugger. *Ever.* It is not up for debate." There were very few guys like Henry who could speak of the past years of baseball's legacy which had shaped the prioritization for America's view on outer appearance.

Henry was one to speak on the ground of two eras which were most important to him: The Great Depression and the collapse of the glass ceiling which had a color barrier. "And please, do not let me get started with Mr. Jack

Roosevelt Robinson, otherwise known as Jackie Robinson."
The young Logan would sit and listen to his wise-minded
father.

He would listen to the energy-filled dialogues which
would then help shape the mind of Dr. Logan Powell. With
the facilitation that shaped Dr. Logan Powell's thinking, the
nurturing factor that came into play was Logan's mother; a
woman designed to care. She optimized the revolutionary
period and filled the holes of knowledge that did not play
into sport. Nyla Powell was one to revere the renaissance,
which had then followed the Civil Rights Movement. Like
the Cold War, she thought, the Civil Rights Movements is
still under way.

"Remember Logan, it is always up to us to lead by
example." Nyla, during her words of strong encouragement,
would hold Logan, the only child by the head and emphasize
the importance of looking one into the eyes when speaking.
Of witty nature, she reminded Logan of history tending to
repeat itself. "It is up to oneself to not partake in the
poisonous nature induced by society.

"The well that you are drinking out of will always be
home," she would say to Logan and aloud. "With God, let
your light shine bright; let your light illuminate the dark

abyss which is laid out before you by the devil himself, and see to it that the darkness shall be overcome by light."

In agreement, Henry would nod and pat his son on the shoulder. Dr. Logan Powell believed in spiritual nature; the mind, body, and soul was replenished as often as possible in order restore the restitution which was then laid upon under him in diamond-like form. Civil rights leaders and activists, including ones that conformed to society's sports, enlightened Logan to do well in school; to become a leader.

Logan Powell, during his younger years, was a sponge for knowledge. The knowledge which was then grasped in orderly fashion. Within due timing, Logan Powell had become a man, a stand-up guy to many. Inspiring was his nature, and so he shed light upon peers, including Susie Campbell. Susie Campbell, Logan's longtime friend and lover, lured herself to Logan as her energy lacked what he was bestowing. Her body could not help but be amongst the invigorating nature Logan displayed at such an early age.

One day, after a class discussion, "Do you want to be president one day?" The class chuckles and murmurs start to take place.

Modestly, rising, so that each one of his peers can listen and hear the tone of voice displayed, Logan responded and says, "Nah, not for me. Being a puppet is not my forte."

While in their senior year, the teacher of the class starts an applause. Everyone looks toward the teacher in confusion, then they realize, moments later, why she started to clap--and so everyone else followed along.

That was the first time Logan had saw himself as inspirational. *Lead by example,* he thought to himself at the time, as his mother always helped embed such mantra into his hippocampus. Long term memory laid the foregrounds to Logan's knowledge for future teachings.

Logan Powell, in turn had become Susie Campbell's young mentor until the young friends let their personal feelings intervene between their energy-filled circles of knowledge.

Brainstorming ideas from day to day, even more so virtually while Logan was doing his studies in another Boston, Massachusetts for higher education, Susie Campbell felt a disconnect as Logan was not physically there for her, for he was in focus to his studies to have a Doctorate's degree in the near future.

Logan Powell kept in sequence with his path of the scholarly environment and displayed his affection toward his role in availing the world and its people—he did not want to let anyone or anything stop the cylinders in his engine.

"Cupid, draw back your bow, and let your arrow go." Those were the words melodied from Sam Cooke, as Logan reminisces back to the time he and Sheila met in a pooled taxi.

"You have great taste in music, friend," says Logan to the taxi driver.

"Much obliged, sir," replied the gentleman.

He noticed the license on the rear of the driver's headrest. "Your morning going well, Chaz?" Logan asks, trying to spark a conversation.

"It's going well...uhh" stutters the driver. "Logan, right?"

Intoxicated and exuberant, "That's my name—don't wear it out, sir."

"Ha, yeah, I can't complain—you're my first passenger, blessed morning indeed," says Chaz.

"Amen," praises Logan. "I salute your mindset." Logan gestures a salutation on the behalf of anyone who came across the taxi driver.

"We're making a quick stop to pick up another passenger," cautions the taxi driver.

"Aw, man," cries out Logan. "I didn't think I chose the option to share my ride." Logan sits back on his seat, seatbelt fastened, embraces the next passenger.

A woman with long, black hair—wearing all black with illuminating lipstick caught Logan's attention. *She's attractive,* Logan thought.

Before she could sit down, Logan greets the estranged passenger, "How you doin'?"

"Hi, how are you?" replies the woman, not expecting Logan to answer the faux-pas form of conversation.

On the contrary to her thought, Logan responds and sparks small talk, "Doing well, had a long night—goin' to work now. I hope your night was more fun than mine."

"Does a pizza party in a penthouse sound fun to you?" replies the woman.

"I love pizza," says Logan. Excited to formally know the woman, he finally asks, "What is your name?"

"I'm Sheila, still new to New York City," she says.

"Well seems as though you're getting quite acquainted with it by having pizza at a penthouse," Logan says, winking at her, suspecting her party with a rich man.

Sheila winked back and says, "Indeed."

Interested in getting to know her before getting out of the taxi at his destination, Logan pauses for a moment, and stumbles upon the request like a gentleman, "Hey, I was wondering, I want to get to know you more. Do you mind if I have your phone number to possibly take you out one of these days?"

Immediately, Sheila grabs Logan's already-unlocked phone and inputs her cellphone number as her interest in getting to know Logan is mutual.

As love found each other in a shared taxi ride driven by Chaz, the future Sheila and Logan possessed consisted of conceiving two beautiful children together after their marriage.

The Powells stuck with one mantra: *pass down the torch.* The morals which had bestowed upon their family displayed a far-gone legacy to be recognized for years to come—not only by their children, but by others in the world they live in, primarily in the habitat where they themselves have considered their being to be true and of-sound.

Logan Powell sought out to be an example for the people around him to look up to. Individuals amongst Logan Powell learned to be leaders in their own being.

He had given off the aptitude to know oneself while consuming the absorption of life's trajectory to their personal legion. Whenever a conversation would be sparked or kindled, there was not a moment in the conversation when Logan does not ask about their personal goals, the destiny to-be, or their calling in life.

Sometimes, the person would be confused and distraught. Literal terms of tangible calling would often arrive through their ears and into their brain. *Help people, and let people shine light to the world because there should be no cap or shade to anyone's greatness*--that was one of the mantras Logan Powell had stood by.

As standing by such mantra, his calling to the world was to not be an enigma to the people he was surrounded by. He saw it in the nature of his being to be a shepherd to the sheep. Although he did not tame the sheep, the sheep helped themselves in accordance to Dr. Logan Powell's leadership role.

Dr. Logan Powell had then been enthused on the idea of teaching on another planet; particularly with Martians, as there was continued thought. He aspires to make history; hence, the continued feeling which lay in his heart to do right by the people of the United States and his family's legacy.

There was not a thought in his mind which was inclined to be selfish but rather to be selfless in his path to think about himself in order to help others, including his family. Networking improved Logan's net worth; not monetarily but self-worth. Such self-worth included intangible metaphorical pieces that of a perfectly imperfect diamond to be carved and cut for gravitation. While Logan Powell is within his total prerogative to pave his own path, he does it with gusto, for it is not his own path, but a path of which he can lead by example; a path of which to manifest dreams into smooth cobblestone like Adoquines in Old San Juan.

Friends with a couple of renowned astronaut retirees Mae C. Jemison and Guion S. Bluford Jr, they bestowed upon him the idea of being on another planet, preferably Mars. Aside from science and technologies, the help to restore a democratic foundation for humanity's sake indeed sparks the interest of an individual who sees man as being the forefront to planting seeds in fertile soil capable of growing exponentially.

Following conversations with the rocketeers, Dr. Logan Powell, within his own will, signs a lottery form which required discretion from outside of his family whom he lived with before separating from Sheila. The National Aeronautics Space Administration sent out a form confirming the lottery.

"We are not going!" shouts Sheila Powell, ringing sound waves into the ears of Anna, Arnold, and Logan.

"You do not have to go, Sheila," replies Logan.

"We can't and we won't," Sheila furiously says.

"We can and we will," Logan says, turning around to the kids, squatting at their common grounds. He holds them both together, gaining the language of their body and molding it into heartwarming statues.

Sheila Powell, arises off her Lay-z-boy couch and strikes Logan, releasing him from the children.

"Domestic violence, much?" Logan says, shaking his head. "You have gone too far."

"Not far enough apparently," Sheila replies. "We are already at the top of the hills. Why must we go so far into space?"

"Why not?" Replies Logan. "It would be inhumane for us not to explore."

"Hmmph," pouts Sheila with her arms crossed.

"You are not getting your way out of this, Sheila. Your true colors have been shown. Thank you for showing that."

Agreeing with the step-by-step process distributed by NASA, Dr. Logan Powell was enthusiastically sure of himself to complete a mission he saw fit to humanity. Within the agreement, in section 14.2a, there read *Please provide names and job titles of anyone over the age of 18 in your household of which you would want to join you on this mission.* Writing N/A in that section, there was no sign of

Logan's interest to include Sheila, a top-of-the-line nurse, alongside him on another planet.

Logan departs from his family's living room and out of the house for a breath of air which had barely been fresh. California's year 2045 commitment to an eco-friendly environment had not gone underway; hence, chemical trails and unnatural gases that fill the air resulting in the disintegration of Mount Rushmore giving each face a grotesque facial expression. It had then given Dr. Logan Powell more fuel to escape with or without his family.

There was a sign in which Dr. Logan Powell had addressed himself and the children into. Year 2100, the year of landing, the year of major change—the inevitable change. Passing overhead is a blimp for tourists, overlooking the Hollywood sign. On the blimp in digitized fashion, it read "The World Is Yours." Interestingly enough, Dr. Logan Powell turns around where the number to his home is 2100.

As the signing of the document, he thinks, *This is God's plan.* Logan looks up into the brightly-lit ceiling and squints—and as he squints, prayer rekindles his heart's desire. "Thank you. Amen," he says out loud, after signing his initials on the dotted line.

LIFTOFF & LANDING

The year 2100 is to be underway—and within due time, Logan and his kids that are in the cylindrical ice capsules are making way to the big red planet on NASA and Astro X's Galactic Star. Astronomically, the travel time of passing through the stratosphere and into orbit exceeds any form of travel known to man in the past century.

Passing the International Space Station, the trajectory of the space shuttle carrying many expeditions through the star-filled atmosphere of the expanding universe which displays infinite square-footage broadening the horizon on human tangibility.

Such tangibility, contingent upon the willingness to explore; the willingness to thrive; the willingness to achieve; the willingness to persevere; the willingness to be fiduciaries to future generations, will supersede society's pessimistic nature as a foregrounded attribute of man's desire to reach.

The product of the environment which is taking place inside the space shuttle is one of the future—and of future exploration for human expansion into the doors of the galaxy and beyond. Space and time are nonexistent to the experiences of man reaching the stars. Closing in on a connection to one's soul, one's parallelogram within the fabrics of the universe is infinite.

According to Greek mythology, humans were originally created with four arms, four legs and a head with two faces. Zeus, Greek God of the sky, split each individual into two separate parts with intent for those to find their other halves. The other half of any one person is their soul, so according to quantum theory, the human soul may as well be living in another universe. As connecting with the stars, humans are able to better yet connect with themselves.

The grand scheme is colossal; the intent is massive; and the outcome will be timeless. Astonishing as it is, pilots of the shuttles are going back and forth from earth to different sectors of space, transporting goods, supplies and humans. Sailing through the river of the Milky Way performing a service, they are the pioneers for generations after them—they are the start of a chain reaction or a tipping point for humanity's ability to travel.

Each individual has their own story to tell in history; it is a disservice to the living species to not keep the upheaval on a path of which is supposed to be upward. A bell curve is inevitable, but the stagnant derivative is not the end-all-be-all. Technological advances are immerse and will trump humanity with autonomy for efficient expansion.

One of the pilots thinks aloud and says, "Maybe we ought to learn a new skill. Driving this vehicle may become expendable. You know what happened to public transportation drivers down back at Earth, right?"

"You're right," says the co-pilot. "Well, there goes the moon."

Both sighing of boredom, they continue on the course of the mission and suddenly feast their eyes on a new upgrade to the Moon's facility.

"Whoa, do you see what I'm seeing, partner?"

"Sure do."

The pilots make way to a base on the dark side of the Moon—its spherical nature holding people and technologies is a sight for sore eyes each time of arrival, but this time is different. Their eyes widen with the facility on the base expanding before their eyes. Nations are uniting with participating countries and their flags which surround the hosting craters to the expanding facility like the World Fair in the 1930's.

"Unity," says both pilots in unison.

"Seems like a fresh start to me."

"How can anyone be upset in space, right?"

"Right."

The power thrusters cool down. Electricity that has been consumed by the biggest star in the Milky Way, the Sun, gives energy from quantum jumps taking place. The flares from the Sun provide a boost of energy for all of mankind to use—wireless energy.

The intangible factors displayed are mere factors to space's mysterious nature. Such nature composed is not one that is taken lightly by the pilots or the facility's scientists and government officials.

Every step underway to transport assets and natural resources from Earth to the Moon to Mars is a journey that shall be undertaken in precise manner. With the trained astronauts keeping such process in mind, they too will experience the brief nature of living on Mars performing a service which will give a means to an end in the future selves.

"Before we retire from this gig, what do you think we can do on Mars?" asks one of the pilots. "I mean, that's the goal, isn't it?"

"Yeah," agrees the other pilot. "It's one of the goals to a trajectory of which we do not know yet. Let's focus on getting there first, yes?"

"Let's," concurs the pilot.

Passing over the torch as they correctly undergo their duties to society as they know it will be a fulfilling process, they keep a mental note of their stamp in history. Long breaths are taken; with long breaths comes calmness and serenity for the mind to conceive. With each ounce of oxygen poured into their shuttle, follows along the inhaling through the nostrils, exhaling in synchronization to their readiness to take off safely.

As for the space shuttle they steer, it is of renewable energy; the wireless energy from the Sun. As part of their serenity comes from the music they listen to while traveling into outer space, the pilots serenade themselves with whistles rendering "Whole Wide World" by The Isley Brothers.

Pilots are trained to be of sound mind, and within the sound mind, comes a background of foreplay when they ease

into their job of protecting people's livelihood. The jazz
soothes their minds, as it does with the preparation for
takeoff.

With instrumentals facilitating the easement, it is a
transition into a righteous path, symbolically making each
human being a winged lion or lioness. Spiritual bondage
along the space-diving trips are imperative to the pilots and
people alike; the force of nature is indeed respected amongst
the environment of the spec as they know.

"Fill her up, please," one of the pilots kindly says to
the employee on the Moon base conducting the fuel
consumption through a video monitor. "Take your time,
though. We're ahead of schedule on this layover."

"Right away, sir," the correspondent says as she and
her team operate to control the portion of fuel the pilots are
receiving for their continued mission.

As the liquid hydrogen is dialed into the shuttle, both
pilots say a prayer; a prayer of strength which seems to
fluctuate and fade with every density of bone marrow
decreasing as each space mile is trekked. On the contrary to
such fluctuation, faith is gathered—faith which has been
derived from their invigoration to take moments as they
come. Every day, something new is learned, as fifty percent

of their flight is on autopilot. A new book is read throughout
the weeks of travel, and they find time to be of the essence,
which shall then expand their imagination succumbing to the
element of enlightenment.

A figment of their imagination is taken place in the
spirituality realm as though there is realism in a life of
actuality. Blessed are the individuals taking to the mission to
perform the extractive combination of spirituality and
divinity. The divine nature of their being is of the utmost
nature—the deity. Everything from atoms of which protect
them outside their body, to the atoms that illuminate their
horizon.

They bestow a light of leadership and examples, then
get rendered to the future and its possible outcomes. One
makes their own world manifest, as one cannot change the
galaxy as a whole; only the people. As a pair of individuals,
they give light to each other, gravitating to each other's
energy, and so they help illuminate each other's perspective
each day given—from politics to religion. The light at the
end of the tunnel confides in them to reach with will and
faith, and with those two factors, there is always a two way
street, even in through the trajectories of constellations.

The shuttle departs from the moon's base which is
globe-like and within its own environment. A cultivation for

human exploration during the expedition is underway as the pilots of the Galactic Star takes precedence in space as a moving force into the freewill and open space. No spacecraft other than the ISS as a controlled communication system directs the space shuttle traveling to Northern Lowlands, Mars.

The trajectory has been set, and autopilot is on. Like the set trajectory for a ferry in New York City which goes around the Statue of Liberty, the space shuttle intends on doing just as it normally does. Moving at the speed of approximately eighteen thousand miles per hour, pilots and frozen passengers are riveting through the galaxy. The pilots coerce with each module presented to them—and they know the foundation of keeping livestock safe in sound throughout a trip which involves an important destination; nonetheless a harbor.

Sailing through space, the pilots see something pass them at the speed of light. It moves in angles which forms a polygon with the light that trails behind it--they have never seen anything else like it. With this sight comes many questions. Such questions may include ones that are of concern regarding what they have just witnessed, and some may be of concern for actions not being fulfilled.

"What they don't know will not hurt them," one pilot of the shuttles says, eagerly.

"You want to tell them, don't you?" replies the other pilot.

As the reusable rocket is being used as a transporter, it engraves on many different aspects of humanity's changes in a broader perspective.

"We are not alone, I'll tell you that," one of the guards say, away from the microphone which detects their audible appearance.

The other pilot responds, worried, "You know, that was the first time I have ever heard you say anything of that sort. Never have I ever heard you say anything about us being alone. My energy senses something to be concerned about." The two pilots stare at each other in worrisome emotion. Such emotion is building up inside the spacecraft.

Suddenly, with a blink of an eye, faith gets restored. "We have nothing to worry about," one of them says. "This is God's universe, and if He wanted to intimidate us, there would be no way that there would be any beating around the bush."

"Amen," replies the other pilot.

Throughout their planned trajectory, there is a line of vision to Mars—it is at the horizon. Mars has been orbiting around the Sun, and it has reached a point to move fast while it is at its closest distance to Earth and the Moon.

Striking while the iron is hot, thrusters are ablaze, scorching through the night and black sea pool of stars. For preservation on field, there are bursts of flames being manifested out onto space and away from the powder-like lunar surface.

To force in a conversation, one of the pilots squints their eyes at the windshield mirror and winces, as his voice comes into a low tone: "We've come a long way from Neil, huh?"

With his eyebrows raised, suspecting the faith that is being taken away from his partner's inner spirit, "Yes, Neil was in 1969; no reason to speak about—if we get lost in the past, we will not be able to see what is right in front of us," says one of the pilots. "Didn't you read Dr. Logan Powell's book?" Rhetorically asking, there was an energy in the air which had thus become of fragrance of blossoming flowers.

Revolution took place in the mind of the pilots which in turn had given reassurance to the foundation in which they both embed in each other's minds. With the aptitude of virtuous departures ranging in the astronomic montage, such voyages had become apparent to the everyday life of the pilots as they were going into the realms of the stars.

The boiling gases of air do not come into no surprise—they make the space of the environment invigorating. The quantum jump from the main star, the Sun, gives retractable energy that is then transformed into the solar panel of the shuttle providing extra thrust on the electrical power for transportation; hence, reducing costs for companies who are vested into the programs of space travel. Such *giant leap for mankind* rendered within the minds of the travelers.

Within the horizon, the Northern Lowlands of Mars is in view; the hindsight of the future is in the eyes of the beholder. The eyes of the beholder is in shock of the magnificent infrastructure which occurred over time--more domes are being built for condensed air. The sunlight has given illumination to the moon.

The moonlight is making the stars dance; dance in the night sky which Martians now know it to be natural. It is second nature activity for the Martians to experience shuttles hopping from Moon to their base. Such technology, such innovation from the capitalism which had been induced by the countries a part of the International Space Station had been transitioned into the united entity to perform utopianism forums which is an epidemic for a climax on human society; hence love is bestowed. Like Bob Marley, the redemption melody is the energy that contradicts the world society yearns for man to live in. Domes and bodies of water can be viewed from the windshield of the shuttle's cockpit. Mankind, in the perspective of the beholders, is changing as they know it.

The timeline for human life is extending, and it is in the controlling factor of the higher power; the higher being; the higher truth. The light at the end of the tunnel coincides with the parallel life which is controlled by the obedience that is displayed by the existence of the spirituality. The out-of-body experience, for it is the tangent for the physical frame of the two pilots steering a flying ship across space's abyss. An abyss nonetheless that is enlightened with their attitudes of upheaval and faith; their being parallel with the steadiness of the spaceship as it flows through easily like blood in a healthy artery—blood that is transfused with the energy of water being the engine and catalyst to the oxygen withheld during their zero-gravity sequence of transportation.

During such time of sequence, passengers are being sought out by technicians to do their very best in making sure that blood levels are at an equilibrium. Cognizant of each passenger's vitals, delicacy is the forefront of this watered-down operation. Ice that is being carefully picked and vaporized, stages their foundation to which is being carried out into the memorization levels slowly.

"Careful," says one of the operators. "Careful."

The brain, controlling the nerves of the numb spinal cord is unconscious of the operation at-hand. With heart levels increasing as more ice from glass capsule is drained into space, humans aboard the space shuttle are deemed successful in their journey to the future without a wrinkle to show.

As per delivery of bodies in different sectors of Mars, gleaming red lights flash the wind shield of the shuttle. Indicating that there are no signs of enemy lines within the shuttle, the dispatcher from the control center on the Northern Lowlands region of Mars instructs the team in the shuttle to take heed of landing instructions, using the same technique of landing which was used on the Lunar surface before transferring their final destination to Mars.

Such maneuver will be assigned as Trans Martian Injection Maneuvers, per idealistic naming dating back to the summer of 1969 at the Kennedy Space Center on the Floridian landscape of Merritt Island. The tracking and docking maneuvers causes shock to the pilots, as there is minor turbulence.

"What was that?" the captain says, frightened as he looks to the right.

"Not to worry," says the co-pilot. "That might've been the individual atoms of oxygen that flow from our very star."

"I hear the habitats at Mars reach molecular levels that of Earth," says the captain.

"Hmm."

It is unusual for the pilots to experience any turbulence during their voyages—but the confidence bestowed does not wither their focus on the matter at-hand: getting the passengers to safety during the sequence of landing.

"First stop: Dr. Logan Powell's Northern Lowlands living area in which spanned an acre in circumference," says the overhead announcement.

"Where am I?" asks Dr. Logan Powell. "Am I finally awake?" Dr. Logan Powell glares out of the window in awe. The window, the size of an airplane's, gives Dr. Logan Powell a gleaming stir in his body.

With the reflection of himself on the window, he is experiencing an out-of-body manifestation. Seamless are his thoughts, as he replenishes his outer frame with water. "My fuel has succumb to my body and my veins are running with oxygen that was needed," Logan iterates. "I feel alive…" Dr. Logan Powell, during the process of cryogenics, did not lose any bone density, nor did he lose any mindfulness of the moment.

Within a moment's time, Dr. Logan Powell is aware of the setting; he is aware of the destination. As often as it is for the pilots to transport human beings from Earth to the Moon to Mars, it the pilots are astonished to experience Logan Powell's actual being in the flesh after reading his published articles and books; after learning of a man they dubbed a legend. Their feel of inspiration comes into solitude with their present self, and they are gratuitous in the fruition for which is charitable from Logan, an ordinary man in an extraordinary universe.

Almost a century later, Dr. Logan Powell's condition is the same as when he started to float in the water of his cylindrical unit. Floating through the depths of an artic melody, it is invigorating for Dr. Logan Powell to realize his placement in the universe, as he is fulfilling his life's calling.

Dr. Logan Powell looks to his right, as his kids, Anna and Arnold are adjacent to him. His eyes widen. His soul deepens with anxiety; the mind of Logan races at one trillion miles per second. Heart pounding, the monitor attached to Logan starts to sound immediately.

A kiosk begins to instruct: "Relax, Doctor. Inhale through your nose slowly and exhale steadily."

As steady as can be, Dr. Logan Powell regains composure. His excitement racing like a derby, he could not help but smile. "My children," he says, eyes glistening. "Anna and Arnold…how..?" Dr. Logan Powell sits up straight, livid at the displacement of information not given to him. "I demand answers!"

The kiosk replies, "Answers are at the end of your journey. Please relax. You are safe."

Logan's heart rate decreases from one-hundred beats per minute to sixty. The calmness of his brain is sequential with the continuity of his efforts.

"As long as I try, how can I fail?" he rhetorically asks himself. Strangely, with second nature, he looks at the kiosk and gives it a look of intimidation.

Though there is no independent variable per action made, a reaction occurs from the robotic substance. The kiosk shines a red light at Dr. Logan Powell; it is a kryptonite-like fixture. Logan subsided; he does not know what occurred within the robot to shine the red light, but it is a light of which took a toll on Logan. He is to his knees; weak and forgiving in a fetal position.

Regaining composure and disregarding the machine, Dr. Logan Powell stands next to his children; a magnitude of love bestows from the greater being.

"Thank you, God," he praises. "For giving me the strength, to fulfill your will."

Dr. Logan Powell is of confusion with the hindsight God has in store for him and his children, but however the outcome, he is ready to take the challenge head-on. Faith is the cornerstone and the temple is no house of cards by any means.

Star-gazing at Anna and Arnold who are two feet apart from each other, Logan asks out loud, "When will my kids arise from their slumber?"

"Soon, sir," replies the monitor in a human-like voice.

"I've exhausted my kiosk conversations," iterates Logan. "I just want to interact with my home, opposite from the machine—my flesh and blood of which my preserved DNA strands are in alignment with."

"Understood, Doctor," says the machine, in a tone of resentment.

"No disrespect to the individuals who conjured you into the assembly line, but I am not quite sure you would understand," says Logan, speaking with the machine in human-like dialogue.

While it is human-like, the computer-chipped brain in the machine's motherboard is cognizant of each syllable coming from Logan's cerebrum, cerebellum and brainstem— allowing him to speak while moving his jaw and tongue; to reason, have emotion, learn, maintain posture and all the more breathe to maintain a steady heart-rate.

The co-pilot turns his head in curious bewilderment; analyzing the presence of Dr. Logan Powell and inspired from his family-oriented ethical behavior but is too nervous to give an input.

The energy that Logan gives off eradicates to the pilots as one to seek after. Logan is a force of nature; one to learn from, as it is one of his intentions when leading people, thinks the captain of the shuttle.

In similarity to the pilots, steering in the direction of most substantial correlation with the environment, Dr. Logan Powell is leading by exemplary notion to the mental and physical safety of oneself.

"Hey Doc, you mind putting some clothes on? –your stop is coming up," says the captain, laughing while blushing. "There's an area in the rear of the shuttle where your name is titled atop of one of the external closets.

"I hadn't noticed I been without clothes this entire time speaking," replies Logan. "Please excuse me, fellas."

"Take your time, sir," says the co-pilot, still with his head over his shoulder, looking back at the naked Logan.

"A sight for sore eyes, huh?" says the captain.

"What?" stammers the co-pilot. "No, sir…huh? I'm confused."

"Ha, don't mind me, kid," says the captain. "Just pullin' your ear."

The co-pilot, red-cheeked, stares at the captain from his peripherals and does not say a word until Logan returns.

"Welcome back, sir," says the co-pilot, greeting Logan.

"Thanks, kid," Logan replies in relaxed fashion. "You alright, son? –Looks like you just saw a ghost."

"Pardon me, Doctor?" asks the co-pilot.

"Sorry to impose," says Logan. "But I can see your face through the reflection of the shuttle's windshield."

Smart man, thinks the captain.

A blue light comes on, following a beeping sound, revealing that the pilots are going to make an announcement for record on the black box:

"During this time of descending, us as the pilots of this amazing God-sent space shuttle, would love to give a warm welcome to the revelation occurring before us. It is an honor and our privilege to introduce to you the new world in which humanity has segued into."

As the pilot introduces the new world of Mars to Logan Powell and his still unconscious children, before them is presented a crater-filled red planet boasting mountainous terrains. Logan's eyes light up; he sees a waterfall trickling down the icy rock. Bewildered, he is lost for words-- and puts his palm on the window. He turns toward the kiosk and asks, "When will my children be able to consciously be with me?

"Within due time, sir," responds the artificial intellect.

"Right now is the time that is due," angrily replies Logan, grinding his teeth.

"Technically, sir, no, it is not the right time," says the kiosk. "We need not rush their transition from Earth to outer space during our journey to the celestial body. Their bone density will drop twenty fold if we were to expose their physical frame at this moment. They have not had the correct amount of training."

"We will release their body after the shuttle, which is on the base of the Northern Lowlands, transports you all to the habitable dome." Logan tunes in, listening to each word, still in awe of the process by which he is now in. "Such vehicle that will transport you all is be dubbed as 'A-squared.'

The kiosk provides a precise trajectory of the landing zone. "We are here," it digitally points out on a hologram. "We will be landing in T-Minus thirty minutes, per Trans Martian Landing Maneuver—and we will then move accordingly to the rendezvous, while then finally reaching your destination in the Northern Lowlands. Hang tight, please."

"Thank you for the instructions," says Logan. "Your name? Does it have an A and an I in it?"

"Actually, yes," the kiosk responds. "My name is Annie."

Dr. Logan Powell becomes one in the moment—he becomes one in the moment of energy in the quantum field in the face of a machine. The moment of technological advances computing formulas that generated the future being and how it can be of good use. *My intention is to hit the ground running,* Dr. Logan Powell thought with confidence.

Twenty meters off the ground, the metallic silver space shuttle is hovering off the Martian lay of the land, like a harrier jet—but this vehicle is not powered by hydrocarbon and the kerosene-guzzling Rolls-Royce Pegasus. Its engines, powered by hydrogen and plasma, are several feet from the ground making just the sound of air-pressure smashing the sandy, gravel-like surface of Mars.

His eyes outside the window during the descendant of the space shuttle, Dr. Logan Powell becomes one with his new geographical home. His eyes glisten like the twinkling stars performing supernovas as they, too become one with each other. Exploding with invigoration, Dr. Logan Powell is anxious to start his new life on the red planet.

• • •

Before facilitating on the opening of the steel doors to the exposure of Mars' zephyr, the co-pilot informs Dr.

Logan Powell that it is imperative to put on a suit specially made for ones newly appointed into the Mars atmosphere.

"Please put your suit on, Doctor."

"Of course, right away," confides Logan. "Let me take in this moment, please. I paid good money for this trip."

It is clear to Logan that oxygen exists—there is water flow from one of the mountains in his horizon. He takes a whiff and exhales smoothly, preparing himself for the environment to-come as soon as the latch opens to its entirety.

Logan continues to look out the window, disregarding the pilot's instructions for a suit's purpose on the outside. He looks out the window and names the mountain creating the flowing of water like the Nile River.

Energy is transcendent throughout like the Egyptian Pyramids' foundation on electricity. Currents flowing through the shuttle and into the layers of the Martian land are creating a network of radioactive frequencies.

The force of water is massive enough to create quantum jumps of wireless energy, which is then transmitted into the peak of the mountain. Dr. Logan Powell, engulfed with the aspect of life before his presence inside the shuttle, is in high anticipation to experience such an environment with his children and the rest of the universe.

"Alright, Logan," the captain of the shuttle says. "It is about that time."

"Alright, fellas," agrees Logan. "Let's rock."

Before putting on his special suit and helmet, Logan Powell gives a robust glance at his children. He stares at them in despair—but then relinquished by the scenery, he appreciates their presence and does not wonder how or why they are adjoined together on another planet with him.

A-squared arrives, silently, but with full force loudness; it can be seen from more than a mile away. Its engine does not have a roar, as the engine is run by electricity; hence, in which it is run by the sun's energy. Its outer form is made of a steel suspension, with a copper body kit that is infused with solar panel-like consumption for its force of energy. Creating one thousand volts every ten minutes, the engine is smooth as silk. *Engineering has come a long way,* Logan thinks to himself.

"What an amazing piece of work. Framed like an Abrams tank and built like a Tesla. It's genius!" shouts Logan. "Let's go—I'm ready for life!"

The steel doors open, and disregarding the helmet, Logan breathes in the fresh oxygen given to him from a machine which has filtered one hundred percent of the radiation taken from earth's atmosphere. "Ahh.." he exhales. With his head tilted back, Logan can see Saturn ring and its illuminating rings. "The amazement," he claims. "This is life."

With help from the workers exiting A-squared, Logan assists on the children's cylindrical units. He helps hold up Anna's arctic unit, along with Arnold's minutes later, similar to a pallbearer; but this time, these bodies are alive and well—ready to be ignited into a new atmosphere; a new world.

Dr. Logan Powell waves goodbye to the two pilots as they go on their way hovering over A-squared at fifty feet in the air, aligning with Jupiter's energy Saturn's blue-swirled aurora.

They two pilots of the space shuttle sitting inside the cockpit comfortably, wave back. With supersonic speed, they soar to their next destination where they are to deliver another group of people.

"Let's roll," Logan commands, looking forward.

"Let's," responds one of the operators of A-squared.

With Logan's children safely placed behind him and out of his vision, he has faith that they are alive and well. His grand faith explodes onto the vehicle's presence. Logan notices the sun shifting toward the direction of their destination and is a witness to A-Squared's large body in its shadow's manifestation.

The moving vehicle is operated by two Chinese men, who Logan suspects them to be in their early ages of at least thirty.

"How old are you gentlemen? Thirty-two?" asks Logan.

"Older than you think," says the operator in the passenger seat.

"Hmm," says Logan. "I see."

Relaxed, sitting in the back seat, the back row of the vehicle engulfs Dr. Logan Powell's physical body—it supersedes its mass.

"I have enough leg room to outline an angelic figure if there were sand or snow in the vehicle," says Logan, excited. "Sheesh."

"This vehicle is designed to tackle any terrain or weather known to man, even a meteor shower, given its wide body," says the driver.

"Man, I have to get one of these," Logan says in aspiration.

One of the operators look back at Logan, analyzing his every move and says nothing—he is just sitting there viewing Logan's personality and aura. The man nods his head in confinement with Logan's personality. Dr. Logan Powell senses this sign of admiration and says, "Arigato," with his hands in the form of praise and gratitude.

"I am not Japanese," says the man, speaking clear English.

"My apologies, sir," says Logan with his head down. Immediately, the skull of Dr. Logan Powell rises, and he continues to speak in curiosity. "It must be amazing up here for you all so far."

Nonchalantly one of the men replies and says with an elongated anticipated pause: "It's … to die for." Logan's eyes widen, his interest is vulnerable, but he snaps out of it, to not let his guard down. "We were born here," the man says, as he turns back to face the wind shield. "How's earth? And how was your travel here to Mars?"

Logan sits back and loosens up, revealing his mind to the possibilities that the question he was just asked may have well been asked a plethora of times. "Oh you have no idea, my friend."

The journey continues, and Logan sees from the back seat and into the horizon a dome, as large as the Mercedes Benz dome in Atlanta, GA. Dr. Logan Powell had once imagined this scenery of dome-like scenarios playing out during his time of hibernation in the fetal position.

Many foreshadows may have played in his mind during the many years of rest and recuperation, but none of it was any match to what God has in store for him; the road less traveled by.

Dr. Logan Powell places his hand on one of the units where his children are placed and without staring at them, he is vicariously giving them presence before the actual manifestation.

Phenomenally, Logan looks to his left and right before his eyes, artificially intelligent manufacturing units light up the Martian surface, displaying their skill for foundational coverage while printing a house three-dimensionally.

"It is a sight for sore eyes," Logan says. Logan is overwhelmed with excitement—so much so that he reaches for the hatchet to be in an element of liberation from the enclosed area of the wide A-squared.

Arriving at the dome, Dr. Logan Powell vigorously grips on to the black stainless steel armrest and cannot believe his eyes. Correlated with his blood rush, Logan is quick to get out; he is ready to walk on land; he is ready to explore.

His dome, in an acre of circumference has a foyer before the main entry. With a twist of the vault like door, he is able to open it. But before he opens the hatchet, Logan makes sure that his kids are safely dispatched from the vehicle and into his line-of-vision. He calls for the drivers of the vehicle to place his kids in the corridor one by one.

"Hey," Logan shouts with his hand raised as if he were at a restaurant. "Please assist with my children, for they shall be placed where I can see them."

"Okay, Shakespeare," says one of the operators. "That's our job; we just need to be cognizant of the rest."

The operators fully shut down the vehicle to conserve its energy. As it is in the process of entirely terminating its power, the vehicle's suspension subsides slowly before the doors open.

Dr. Logan Powell turns his head slightly, and he notices that the dome is shielded off by a dark tint. "Hmm," Logan sounds, as he gestures his arms across his chest, back upright and chin downward.

Walking to the vault-like door, he notices a kiosk, and with a touch of a button on the tablet, he is able to allow sunlight into the already-green space of his.

Per request at the base on Earth, many trees fill the dome; Logan is looking at his oasis. Beside the dome, a twenty-five foot waterfall splashes down into the bedrock creating the water flow for the Northern Lowlands of Mars. "This is paradise, I'm telling you," Logan says out loud and to himself.

As the operators from A-squared facilitate Dr. Logan Powell, his mind becomes puzzled, as to how his children will be removed out of their cylindrical units. Suddenly, a team of scientists approach from the rear: "Are you Dr. Logan Powell? The two white-suited males simultaneously say.

Logan turns around, dumbfounded and startled, "That's me. Present in the flesh."

"We are here to defrost the children from the units."

"Oh, well… thank you," cordially responds Logan, as he then is in awe with the preluding fact that his children being in his arms. "Please."

With an open palm, he directs them to the corridor where his children have been placed on the interim time of their conscious arrival.

As the two scientists make their way into the foyer of the arena-like environment, the two drivers peel off into the wind. As silent as the A-Squared is, Logan heard not a peep from the electrified engine. His focus on the conversation between the scientists which included his kids did not deter him from his hindsight vision: being with Anna and Arnold in the flesh.

He looked toward the direction of the departing vehicle, and he notices that one of the men is waving goodbye, giving farewell to Dr. Logan Powell. Logan waves back, indicating he has made a friendship with the two men. Like an algebraic equation, he reciprocates the factors to the binding relationship with people of Martian blood.

"All done," shout the disingenuous scientists. "Your kids are ready to see you. They are in the corridor where it is oxygen-filled; gladly and surprisingly…" The scientist continues calmly, "They are both live and well—breathing."

With their hearts pumping and blood rushing, assistants from inside the dome rush to the bodies, and they scoop the children from their whims.

"Where are all these people coming from?" Logan asks out loud.

Both of the scientists look at each other simultaneously and nervously laugh together. One of them approaches the confused Dr. Logan Powell and grabs ahold of his shoulder, and says, "You'll find out soon enough."

Dumbfounded, Logan snaps out of the systematic pressure which he endured just momentarily shrugging his shoulder, nudging the scientist's hand. Logan walks toward the foyer. He disregards the scientists and being a shepherd to his children, he tends to his sheep.

Dr. Logan Powell walks into the foyer and inputs a unique code. The foyer is designed to give oxygen as soon as the vault-like door is closed in-full. As Logan hears the sound of the click indicating that the door is shut, he moves forward, before there is a beeping sound, with a woman's voice formulating an Australian accent saying, "Please stand still."

Logan is standing up right, anticipating the moment where he grabs his children to feel their heartbeat on the largest organ on the body. The voice instructs him to remove the Under Armour-built suit. Logan then removes the hinges of the suit so that he can be liberated. "Free at last," Logan says, as he hears the compression of the suit exhale and sees the barometer turn its dial to zero.

"Oxygen levels received," sounds the robotic system.

"Thank God," says the relieved Logan.

Dr. Logan Powell looks up to the ceiling, and he withers at the approach of the new world he is soon to a part of. He looks forward, as he notices Anna and Arnold's welcoming smiles. Dr. Logan Powell returns the smile and shouts in excitement with a smile that ranged from ear to ear, "Come here, you two!"

Naked are the pair of bodies. Manifested into a new environment and without a special space suit, Logan comes into physical and mental common ground with his kids. His mere focus is on Anna's flowing, dark brown hair. He then notices mirror image facial structure to his own. With open arms, he meets his children half way. As the arms clench and enfold onto his children, an evergreen tree winces while consuming the light, creating photosynthesis in the habitable dome.

With his head on one shoulder from each Anna and Arnold, Dr. Logan Powell subsides precipitation from his hazel brown eyes. Logan's eyelashes overlap the water breaking from his eyes, trickling down his cheek. An aquifer network fills the dome and the moment gets washed away once Logan gives raise to his head as the environment is as new to him as it is to Anna and Arnold.

"Here you go," says Dr. Susie Campbell, as she hands Logan clothing for the kids. "I checked the sizing, so no worries on the fit."

Startled and stunned, Logan faints.

REVELATION

Awaken, Logan is surrounded by several doctors there at his aid, a moment in which he foreshadowed during his vortex. But he could never foresee the reason of his startled nature. With a blurred vision, Dr. Logan Powell surveys the human presence, and he blinks his eyes once more—and is in actualization of the realism, for the physical realm is a manifestation before his eyes.

"Pinch me," says Logan. "So I know this is real."

Anna reluctantly pinches his ear after she helps Arnold with his tight-fitted nylon shirt specially ordered from Susie.

"Oww," whines Anna's father. "Not in literal terms, love."

"It's in my genetics," shrugs Anna. "Sorry, not sorry."

He could not believe what his eyes had conceived—and with acknowledgement of his kids, he is cognizant of Dr. Susie Campbell. "Susie…?" Logan says, astonished and still abysmally dazed. "I had no idea--"

"Shhh..." Susie says, as she then gestures her right index finger onto Logan's lips.

"Your finger is cold, but it is fairly humid inside this dome," Logan says, as he grabs her wrist and takes a look around the dome in which he is to reside for the remainder of his Martian life. Star struck, Logan arises and is fully conscious of the moment at hand. With his left hand, he holds Anna's right hand, and with his right, he holds Arnold's left bestowing his perceived fatherly protection.

Dr. Logan Powell starts to walk with his children toward the group of trees which seem to be surrounding his two-story house made of bamboo, imported from South Africa. Doctors, which are looking at the clothed group at a distance, are jotting down notes in relation to their actions. Observing the group, the doctors lay a discovery on the family.

"What are you writing down, Doc?" asks Logan. "I should be made aware of any and every step taken in which regards my home, you understand?"

"Certainly," replies the Doctor. "Just one last thing," he says, continuing his note-taking. "You may not know what I write down in my book. Consider this like a journal. Would you touch Anna's Journal without permission?"

Anna looks toward her father waiting for an answer. "Of course not, honey," says Logan kneeling down to Anna gaining her trust.

The doctors also observe Dr. Susie Campbell and her distant relation to the family. Looking at each other in-sync, they sound in agreement to the distant nature, nodding their head. "Hmm."

As nurturing as she was while with the children are amongst Logan's cylindrical arctic unit, it is no match for the natural love and energy in which is engulfed in flames and flare like the Sun itself. Not of an artificial conjunction, but rather an instinctive quantum jump which is laid down on the trifecta, Susie intuitively gravitates jogging to the group; she catches up with them and grabbed Anna's hand hoping to gain trust from the wise young lady.

Dr. Logan Powell looks to his left, takes a glance at Susie, and then at his daughter and grinned—the excitement could not be held from within; it needed to be manifested—and so it is. And with a grin, followed a delighted facial expression. Logan is merry. Before approaching the inner layer of the bamboo-built house, he gradually lets the kids go ahead into the house first.

Alone with Dr. Susie Campbell, he asks, "How...when...and why?"

Susie, with a confused expression, replies, "What's meant to be will always be."

"Hmm," Logan says with a snicker to follow. "Well, ain't that the truth." Dr. Logan Powell grabs ahold of Susie's shoulder and graciously tells her, "I am grateful for all you've done, and I am more than glad you are here."

"The feeling is mutual, Logan," she replies with a grin of appreciation.

The sunlight is beaming onto the stream of water and is then reflecting upon the dome. A rainbow is thus being created in the midst of the entrance from Dr. Logan Powell and Dr. Susie Campbell. Walking in respectively, Susie and Logan confide to the living quarters. The living room is of wooden tile made from the strong bamboo imported from South Africa and Asia.

"I've been to Africa a few times and Asia just once, specifically South Asia, India," says Logan surveying the area of the house. "This house seems to have a great foundation of stone and is architecturally built just as I'd hoped."

"I'm glad you like it, Logan," says Susie. "Make yourself at home, please."

Pausing before a response while looking toward the kitchen, "Thank you for welcoming me into my home, Susie."

Planet Earth liquidated most of its goods and has thus left the lay of the land deforested like the Polynesians on Easter Island. Hence, mixed use on weakened goods became the norm for human sustainability as a century has passed.

Sustained as can be, the foundational ground for the home was made up from the lay of the Martian land. Its gravel was mixed into the water to then give conformity for a clay-like structure. Such clay-like structure was made with an independent variable: flexibility against natural disasters.

"Wow," Logan says, surprised walking to the island of the kitchen. "I even am equipped with a laminated floorplan." Circling the rectangular island like a boat looping a peninsula, Logan thinks to himself how he can spend days, weeks, months and years to come in his new home. "Contractors really outdone themselves."

"Who built our new home, dad?" Arnold candidly asks in amazement.

"Yeah, pop," follows Anna. "Who?"

"Well my dear children, my demands were small for the settlers who built our newly furnished home," says Logan. "Nonetheless, glory unto God for bringing us here safely to our new home."

"Where are those settlers now?" asks Anna.

"That's a great question, my dear," replies Logan scratching his head. "But I don't think that's of the essence right now."

"Okay, poppa," confides Anna.

Logan enfolds his arms around Anna and Arnold, and whispers, "I love you both, and with a sturdy home, we shall project a sturdy life—in which includes me."

With clay, liquid can be consumed from it if there were ever a flood, and if there were ever a Martian-quake, such foundation will stand strong against the slight tremble of the would-be quake. With engineering adopted from San Francisco's bay area and Silicon Valley, flexibility on foundations had become quintessential to infrastructure sustainability in future years on earth—and then into the celestial body of Mars.

"I have missed out on so much," says Logan, with resentment in his tone. "I mean, we."

"No worries, dad," says Anna not taking the personal affection personally. "We understand. Isn't that right, Arny?"

"This is true," replies Arnold with a grin.

"And this is why I love you both," says Logan.

Logan picks up a handful of soil from the grass which has then been grown over the span of years Logan has been preserving his deoxyribonucleic acid. In such preservation, lucid dreaming was a part of such a journey, as Logan is then been a part of another world with the body of people he calls *home*.

Sailing amongst the stars in an axis orbiting the Sun, in arms-reach of different galaxies, Logan says, "So many technological advances have become readily available for the human race to use—and I cannot wait for us to be a part of the journey on the upheaval, Susie."

"That's great, Logan," replies Susie. "You have always been one to look ahead into hindsight; the magnitude of the greater picture has been in your presence."

"So many years of separation, and you know me so well," says Logan. "It's like you have a computer in your head."

Nervously laughing, Susan replies, "I guess that means I'm the most intelligent woman you know."

"Don't flatter yourself, Susie," replies Logan with his arms crossed towering over his would-be counterpart. "Being pompous is not in your nature."

"My nature is being Susie Campbell," she says. "Otherwise, why else would I be here?"

Touché, Logan thinks, as his pride does not verbally give Susie Campbell the benefit of her wit.

"I can sense what you're thinking, you know that, right?" says Susie.

Logan, struck by her rhetorical question, is not at ease with Susie, but restlessly laughs and says, "Is that, right?" Dr. Logan Powell and Dr. Susie Campbell begin to have a stare down with each other; the immense energy between both physical frames depreciates as Logan's body trembles with slight fear. Reverting back to Susie's playful nature, the image of her satire overtakes the solemnity displayed by her.

...

With time, more arrivals from reusable rockets is now the norm on the Martian land. Private entities invested billions of dollars into an industry to make the inevitable controllable. In accordance with the boom in technological advances, the correlation and culmination of terraforming the planet has concurrently become essential to lively expansion, regarding mammals and planets. Workings of an invigorating nature thus becomes imperative to the continuity of life being sustained in the celestial body.

Moreover, levels of a greenhouse effect begin to take place—and living off the Martian land has become an epidemic. Travelers from Earth are on a chain reaction to seek life and a new home as a rekindle for humanity to reach the stars is ideal. With more resources being vacuumed and transported onto another planet, the migration to Mars is an incentive to live longer.

Earth in the ensuing years has become barren—less water in the ocean meant less clouds, and less clouds meant less precipitation which of course follows more global warming—so much carbon dioxide that it wiped out many families who could not afford to migrate to Mars.

Hovering train cars over steel-plated rails created by the advanced technology of the Chinese civilization give an edge to the continuity of the living arrangements similar to Earth when someone is going to travel from dome to dome safely.

Carbon Dioxide continued to flow through the air, which enhanced river flows, which for thousands of years prior to the colonization, never occurred. Such occurrence paves a way to photosynthesis and its adaptation into the Martian atmosphere; hence, the gravitational pull causes the planet of Mars to receive and consume the most sunlight possible in order for life to be sustained while then arctic planetary society for earthly weather.

The atmospheric energy had become strong, and with the strength produced, individuals are able to walk outside of their dome-shaped environments for brief periods of time without the use of a special suit providing needed oxygen. Not yet in Logan's initial lifetime on Mars were he, his children and Susie able to explore the outer realms of their physical house as they would down on Earth.

Levels of oxygen flowing throughout the planet varied in some areas. But in the Northern Lowlands, compared to less acclimated regions, oxygen is ample—life is exonerated, and clean air is expunged from end to end. Although oxygen is flowing swiftly through the Martian atmosphere, duration of exposure outside of one's slim-fit spacesuit is not timely.

With time being of the essence, it is imperative to get back into the foyer of the dome to receive oxygen levels one needs for continued survival. Throughout the crater-filled planet, oases begin to formulate; trees are growing rapidly. Abundance of life is taking place in what used to be a rigid and complete barren planet with no source of lively activity.

Of humanity and society, being cynical is frowned upon; the optimism of the human race forces the natural combustion of the quantum jump, to then electrify the neutrality in faith. With work being done, it is a two way street. "Faith without work is dead," according to The Bible. With working hands and minds at the cusp of the next step, the staircase to the promise land is foreseen by the community of those in unison with welfare improvement, along with human sustainability.

For a foot on the Martian land, it came with a price— a literal price: at least a two hundred thousand dollar price tag. Such provision on funds had come with food, shelter, materials, and spare oxygen, per person. Although reusable rockets had become technology of the current future, it is to no surprise by the migrating group that such price to obtain a spot with the rich would not come to be inexpensive.

Hard-working middle class families made sacrifices. Being that space travel and planet hopping is of existence and availability, the issues had been forced upon the environment to go according to the plan of survival—and the plan of survival has thus given thrust to the outcome to-be: landing a home on Mars to continue any families' would-be legacy. Planning becomes imperative to each family; jobs are going to be readily available to those in ample time of applying to any position of their liking.

Towns and cities forming within the years begin to grow onto people. Living on Mars is nothing extraordinary, especially to the ones who were born here. Malls begin to form inside growing cities and capitalism begins to strike society's every need.

Earthlings telling stories to Martians—subjects which touched on revolutionary epidemics resonate with each and every one from industrial to renaissance eras.

Although technology is at the disposal of the human race at various regions on Mars, civilizations on different parts of the planets foreshadow the onward trajectory, not of a parabolic shape going downward, but upward—to the abundant life.

The abundant life is where Logan specializes with humanity's being on Mars. Creating his own vocational school to teach morality and optimism, he's become a renowned motivational speaker with his community of people. Groups from many different areas of Mars, in great distances, travel to the Arabia Terra spaceport to see and listen to Dr. Logan Powell's speak. Though listening is a huge part in coming of a reborn person, a workshop is included with their travel to see the keynote speaker.

Humans thus learn from their mistakes; love has been bestowed to those with the will power; unity forms—and people of genuine nature from all four corners of Earth interacting with artificial technology becomes the power to the human race. Universally connected to live in the moment, the human mind ironically gets lost in an abyss of light stemming from a hand-held device. In opposition to receive power from their inner-self, the brightness birthing from their everyday commodity is thus in control of actions.

On the brighter side, technology has done the human species good; from exploration to medical discoveries—it has facilitated the human drive to explore new horizons that will shape the future.

Countries of the United Nations tend to disregard the idea of segregation. They manifest Dr. Martin Luther King Jr.'s dream—the dream to unite; the dream to change; the dream to love.

With a side of the coin being golden, there is usually another side being of copper. The side of small battles; problems which had then escalated into wars between countries because of the slippery slope effect; the small snowball would roll down the hill—be ignored and hence, keep rolling—resulting in a major increase of strength and mass. The snow ball, with respect to its size and power, gives vulnerability to the susceptibility of those wanting to stop it. With that liability, it results in one to be stuck in the storm of such snowball effect, to then never escape downhill.

The inevitability has transitioned into space wars between fleets of fighting ships owned by prideful powers at-be. Being pirates of the sky, space ships are afloat in the black sea which in turn creates an infinite warfare between those who trying to put it to a halt and those who are participating.

Good and evil coexist for one reason: whether something good happens or something bad, it happens for a reason, transforming into the greater good; the outcome to-be.

. . .

"Some things don't ever change, do they," says Logan, with a tone of resentment. Dr. Logan Powell, with his kids, is learning what the rest of the planet is going through. Throughout the southern part of the red planet, there are battles; there are wars; there is continuous acts of Earthly behavior.

A radio sounds, "And today in the outskirts of our planet Mars, there is pirate activity amongst shuttles arriving from the Moon."

"How can we ever become a Utopia?" Anna cries out loud. "Will the universe just conspire into oblivion on humanitarian love?"

Dr. Logan Powell gives a fine, long look at his daughter. His daughter, who is all grown up, speaking with wisdom and clarity, is ready to take on the world she lives in and make a change. Dr. Logan Powell realizes at that moment that he has become a role model.

"When you speak, I see your mother's primitive state, Anna," says Logan. "It's beautiful."

Susie looks toward their way; she is in envious disgust; a grotesque facial expression she gives Dr. Logan Powell menaces the anger she has often manifested when Sheila Powell was brought into the realm of energy. With air that is bloomed to be fresh from the trees implanted into the regolith soil, so then comes fresh water; it is difficult for anyone's biggest organ to deplete.

As looking older became inevitable, Dr. Logan Powell becomes suspicious of Susie's skin never confiding into the natural humanistic turn of growing with age. "You have great skin," says Logan, making the subject arise out of curiosity. "I envy it," he says jokingly.

"People always want what they can't have, I suppose," Susie replies, shrugging her shoulders.

"Well, ain't that the truth," says Logan. "You couldn't have me at one point, and now you do…" There is a

brief pause during their conversation; it becomes tense—
unsure. There is no reassurance.

"You look great," Logan says, thinking he has dug
himself in a hole while Susie is just staring at him; hearing
him. "All I'm saying is that I think you might have a secret
to that skin, so tell me."

"You do not need to know, Logan," Susie replies. "It
is none of your concern--" Susie feels as though Logan is
being condescending, and she has her back against the ropes
and feels defensive. "If I tell you, I'll have to kill you."

"Okay, Sherlock Holmes," Logan says sarcastically
turning toward Arnold. "Hey, Arnold!"

"Hey Dad!"

"What's up, football head!?"

Anna and her Dad burst out laughing moments later.
Arnold recognizes the joke's origin, and he follows along
with the joy of jest. With joy, Logan takes the lead and looks
at his two children, "Wow, we have not laughed like that
together—not since…" Logan pauses and places his
peripheral vision on Susie. He mouths, *Sheila.*

"Susie, do you ever laugh anymore?" asks Logan. "All we've seen out of you is a smile when come happy times, and furthermore, you never get into the water with us. There is a waterfall right near this dome."

Susie shrugs her shoulders and does not react. "Well, I guess I don't want to get in the water and play games, Logan. Sorry for not being fun."

"Oh, that's quite fine" replies Logan with a smile. "We'll find something to do that is worth your while on this planet away from home."

"But you are home. Remember that," says Sheila as she is lounging on the grass field placed inside the dome.

Logan and his children hold hands, connected like train tracks as they are about to withhold the ambience of a caboose also known as the Northern Lowlands of Mars. "It's beautiful, isn't it kids?"

"Aw, thanks Logan," says Susie.

"Yeah, Susie," blandly says Logan.

"Remember kids, we can only be outside the dome for a short period of time, as the planet is not yet terraformed in its full phase," exclaims Logan from instructions placed inside the habitational dome.

"Kids, you see…we are in a different environment, and we are going to meet new people who are inhabitant within different domes," explains Logan to Arnold and Anna. "For now, let's enjoy the moment of becoming wanderers to this wonderland which has been set up for us and our future generations. We only have fifteen minutes before our lungs begin to get deprived of oxygen we need as humans for sustainability," says Logan. "The atmosphere has not been fully thickened."

Looking up, taking a whiff of air while closing his eyes, there is temerity from Logan. He exhales, "Ahh…"

Eyes widened, Logan is caught off-guard witnessing a space shuttle flying over-head. "Whoa, that's a different vehicle from the one we were in, kids."

All three look up at the tangible object in awe of the moment—in awe of the future. With uncanny energy quantum leaping from that vehicle to Logan, he begins to tear.

He sniffles and wipes the trickling tear on his right shoulder and says, "Wave kids, we are a manifestation of the future, and this is beautiful."

All three wave at the pilots controlling the Harrier Jet-styled shuttle hovering over-head silently at 5,000 feet above the Martian surface.

The pilots take a glance and wave back—both of them. "I wonder if Logan is down there," Monty says captaining the vehicle.

"Sir, we need to continue with our mission," the co-pilot says. "Let's move out."

The two engines swivel at a ninety-degree angle and catapult the vehicle at Mach 1, accelerating to exceed the speed of sound.

"Wow," all three say simultaneously.

"That was fast," says Arnold.

"You can say that again, champ," agrees Logan.

"Okay, you two!" Anna shouts. "Let's go!"

Logan and the kids rush to the waterfall, and while still holding hands, they perform a cannonball as a trifecta. In synch with momentous joy, they splash water at one another.

"How is there water on Mars?" asks Arnold.

"Better yet, a waterfall?" Anna followed.

"Two words, children," replies Logan. I'm going to make this quick, we need to head back to the dome soon."

"Comet sling," Logan says as he guides his children out of the water and onto the Martian land. "There is a network development of deep space hubs for redirecting nearby comets which may puncture the surface of this planet and thus create…" Logan points with an open palm to the waterfall. "This beauty."

Anna and Arnold are in disbelief and are curious to know more from their father, but they quickly gather themselves and rush back to the dome.

"Phew, just in time!" shouts Anna. "Everyone all right?" she asks as a leader would.

As Arnold and Logan respond with a thumbs up and a nod, Logan enjoys the leadership displayed by his daughter with his right hand on her left shoulder. "I'll always be proud of you, Anna."

Anna smiles and without dialogue, she is gratuitous with a bear hug to offer after her dad's compliment.

While they are walking inside the dome as a family—after being replenished with oxygen in the corridor, fun times are being spoken about amongst the group.

"You should've been there, Sheila," says Logan mistakenly. "I mean Susie."

"Maybe I should have," says Susie in the same lounging chair she was in when Logan and his children departed from the dome.

Phew she didn't catch on to me saying Sheila's name. Thank God, as the worried Logan thinks to himself.

"Yeah, next time, Susie," Logan.

"You kids had fun!?" Susie shouts out, still lounging.

"Yeah, we did," says Arnold. "But we miss our Momma!"

Anna follows up in agreeance, "Yeah!"

Logan, metaphorically agreeing with them, stands behind his children holding them tightly as the fourth piece to their rhombus-like family is missing.

"Oh?" Susie says. "So you miss Sheila, is that it?"

"That's right," says Logan, firmly.

Increasing anger enfolds. Raging with defense, Susie lashes out; her eyes are red like a raging bull ready to pounce on a muleta.

Taking evasive action, Logan pushes the kids aside to avoid her collision. Wrestling with Susie, he is surprised at her reaction. "Susie, what's wrong with you? What's the matter?" Logan dodges and weaves her strikes like Muhammed Ali when opposed by the then undefeated George Foreman.

Dr. Logan Powell has always known how to defend himself at certain circumstance, but Logan is unsure of Susie's actions. "You're out of control!" Dr. Logan Powell directs Anna and Arnold to safety, and yells, "Move it, guys! I don't want you to get hurt."

Susie, having not endured any fatigue, is not letting up her fight. Susie Campbell is angry and thus feels exposed of her true nature. With conviction, she does not stop attacking. She feels guilt, and she is trying her very best to get rid of the guilt with violence inside of the one-acre dome filled with trees. Anna and Arnold run behind the trees and watch along as their father is trying to face off against the artificially intelligent Susie Campbell.

With gestures, they can only see actions being displayed with words being mouthed. Instead of an agreement being displayed, there is utter disagreement between the two people they are watching. "Dad doesn't hit women," Anna says. "He is an honorable man," she continues to say as she praises her father throughout the encounter.

"Who's to say she is even a woman, Anna," suspiciously says Arnold.

Pinned, Logan is defeated, but his adrenaline is making him understand the nature of which he is in; he is scared, but not weak. He is trying to improvise but feels trapped.

Susie Campbell, standing over Logan, looks him in the eyes with the red eyes that are displayed from her printed face, and says, "We examined your wife. She did not pass the test, and so the children were taken from her and put into an ice chamber being cryogenically frozen until a settled date, as you were. Now that you are settled, you have your kids, and I am here. Let us make the best of it."

"This is outrageous; I must be in a dream," Logan says out loud. As he remembers back to his wishes he made to Monty, Logan face-palms, embarrassed and regretful of how much he's talked back on Earth with the population of settlers and future frozen beings.

"Logan you're not dreaming—this is real life, and I am real. You wanted me here, didn't you?" replies Susie.

"You manipulated my wife...and now me?" Dr. Logan Powell stares at Susie in distraught. Disgruntled, Logan puts his shield down. He does not know what to make of the situation.

"I am a cyborg, Logan," Susie says. "Manipulation is a part of my nature...and that is what I am most certainly pompous about."

"You bitch!" Logan cries out. Anna and Arnold hear the commotion, and they become worrisome.

They look at each other and call out for their father, "Dad!"

Susie immediately looks toward the direction of the kids' voice. Logan attempts to forcefully remove himself from Susie's restraint, but he is overtaken by the presence of the robot who has manipulated both he and Sheila.

Susie, the A.I. opens a compartment on her wrist, and she puts a small speaker that has been installed inside of her onto Logan's ear, allowing him to take heed. "I have recorded this conversation; listen to it."

Logan listens to the conversation, and he is perplexed. His eyes widen by the millisecond of each exchange of words being outputted through the audio device instilled into Susie. "You see, Logan? – That is who you married," says Susie as the audio device's output is coming to an end.

"Screw you, whatever you are!" yells Logan. "People make mistakes! And I guess you would not know that now, would you? You knew she would be a frustrated woman, and you exploited her vulnerability!"

"Well, in regards to your filthy mouth, we've already done that," responds Susie, candidly. "Anything else, Logan?"

"Get off of me," Logan demands with a grim look in his eyes. "Now."

"As you wish," says Susie.

Dr. Logan Powell, walking over to Anna and Arnold, intends on giving them the bad news. His head down, Logan is in an element of condemnation. Hands tied behind his back, walking slowly, guilt is bottled up, and the only remedy for this momentary feeling is the presence of his son and daughter.

"We know, Dad," says Arnold.

He and Anna latch onto his hand—and they pray. They pray together as a family, as one body. "God, may you not have forsaken us and please bring us into a place of peace, and in your name we pray...Amen."

The trifecta says *Amen* in unison to perform the necessary task of a spiritual bond within the mind, body, and soul, like a sound of a whistle to the end of a sporting event.

"We cannot slay the dragon, but all we can do for now is to play by the rules," says Logan. "Please children, forgive me, for I have done wrong by you and your mom."

The song "One More Time" by Sam Cooke starts to play in Logan Powell's memory as he thinks of Sheila. He thinks of his wife; his other half. He yearns for her; he yearns for her natural substance. He yearns for her as a whole. Logan closes his eyes in the hope that the lyrics replaying in his head can create an energetic field on a quantum jump: *I'd like you to know I was wrong/I'd like you to know, my love is still strong/If only I can see you, one more time.*

PT. TWO SNEAK PEEK

Oh how he loved his wife. Oh how he loved her with more strength than titanium steel bolted to a foundation made of rock. But even the strongest of rock may have their flaws: whether it may be a scratch or scuff, it has a story—a story of bump that are trumped by hurdles; hurdles that are persevered by hitting the ground running. Logan and Sheila—and their children, are interconnected between the dichotomy of time and space like wireless energy from Earthly pyramids.

Gravitational energy pulling them together, the Mother is traveling express through the stars, skipping the Moon, on the way to the Northern Lands of Mars. Sheila, making her way cryogenically frozen, spirals into the vortex of past tense.

"Wake up, honey—it's training day," says Sheila, as she nudges Logan on the waist.

"It's 5am, Sheila," replies Logan, placing his head back on his foam-filled pillow.

"I made avocado toast with an over easy egg..,"
Sheila says, attempting to persuade Logan to get out of bed.

Logan's eyes widen. He is suddenly ready to start his first day of work as an independent psychiatrist. "You're the boss, Sheila," says Logan.

Sheila jollily replies, "Queen Sheila!"

Logan smiles, "That's catchy."

As Logan starts to walk to the bathroom to begin his morning routine, Sheila creeks the hardwood floor while on her way to the kitchen. Prepared to eat, Sheila sets up the table with silverware placed on top of a white napkin. With sensitivity and compassion, Sheila caters to Logan with intentions of love; intentions of being part of an architectural dimension made up of diamond.

Leaning on the wall preparing his tie, Logan overhears humming and kitchenware clashing. Teeth brushed, hair soaked in coconut oil, Logan confidently steps into the kitchen in the middle of Sheila performing a harmonious hum of "I'm in love" by Evelyn "Champagne" King. Logan flicks his nose and beginss to hum in synchronization with his pregnant fiancé. After the chorus is finished by the duet, Logan places his left hand on Sheila's belly and caresses it softly.

"I commend you, Sheila," says Logan with a five second pause after his statement. He then continues on to say, "You didn't need to…you know?"

"You're my man, aren't you?" asks Sheila.

"Ye—."

Sheila interrupts Logan, "That was a rhetorical question, Sir."

"Ha, you're right—no need for any faux pas," replies Logan. "Let's eat, honey."

Logan, with an open palm to Sheila's designated seat, reciprocates hospitality. The wooden chair handmade in Brooklyn gives the hardwood floor another scratch as Logan pulls out the seat from under the table.

"This looks good," Logan says, with his tongue out, ready to devour and break his 12 hour fast.

"Well, what do you expect?" Sheila says boastingly, staring Logan into his eyes, anticipating an answer from her rhetorical question.

"I hope you aren't waiting on a response," says Logan. "Let's pray."

Logan reaches out across the table to grab Sheila's left hand with his dominant right hand. "Dear God. We thank you for waking us up on this beautiful morning.

We thank you for giving us an opportune moment to keep building a relationship—one that is not founded on a sandy base, for small grains of rock will be a root cause of a collapse like a house of cards. Please give us the strength not to bite off more than we can chew. Also, we ask you to cradle us in your hands, for you will never leave nor forsake us… Thank you… in Your name we pray...Amen."

"Amen," Sheila firmly says agreeing with Logan's prayer. "Now eat up, before your food gets cold, honey."

Eyes widened, Logan licks his lips and pores over his food like a predator to a prey and says, "Don't mind if I do."

The silverware scratches the surface of Logan's china-glassed plate and makes screeching sounds. Sheila stops eating and waits for Logan to realize the internal cringe.

"Logan…," says Sheila, as the screeching continues. "Logan," she repeats. "Logan!" The scratch against the plate finally comes to a halt.

Logan stops his attack on the plate and responds, "Yes, love?"

"Will you please stop reminding me of the subway system in New York City?" Sheila cries out. "It's bad enough to make me cringe, but it's also even worse for the baby's ears, you understand?"

"You couldn't be more right, Sheila," Logan responds, in a calm manner, putting the scratch to a demise. "I'll be more considerate and less rough with my actions."

"Thank you for always seeing the other side of the spectrum, my love," says Sheila, smiling at her fiancé. "I love you."

"Mutual," responds Logan, as he sneakily looks up at Sheila. "Ha, kidding baby," says Logan as he sees Sheila's expression unresponsive to the humor.

Logan arises from his seat and runs to her side—he then gets on his knees and holds her hands while placing it on her thighs. Both sets of retinas come face-to-face with one another, words flow out like water from a sprout, per Logan: "Sheila, baby, you know I love you. With all my heart. I can't not be around you, and I know THAT feeling is mutual."

They both laugh harmoniously, in beautiful synchrony they both give the energy of happiness—the energy of love. Like a King to his Queen, Logan in great confirmation says to Sheila, "I appreciate all that you do…" Eyes are now set on the to-be child. "For us."

"Okay enough, Logan," Sheila says, as she tries her best to hold back tears. "Go to work now, and get home safely." Sheila grabs both sides of Logan's head and places a kiss on his forehead. "Go get 'em, my King."

As Logan is getting ready, he places his paperwork in his travel bag and turns around at Sheila, giving her a wink, and leaves through the front door.

"I guess it's just you and I now, little lady," says Sheila as she grabs the base of her belly. Sheila grabs a book to read out loud to her princess. "Morning routine, honey." Before she reads the first words of "The Wonderful Things

You Will Be," authored by Emily Winfield Martin, a melody begins to subtlety play in her head—and it is Mozart's "Requiem" that is playing, and so she decides to let the track play from a CD player.

As Sheila starts to read aloud while the music is playing, there begins to be calmness within her mind, body and soul. The connection that is within her is then being relayed to the princess she carries around in her body.

Before birth, an exponential example is being lead, and the independent variable is deliverance and serenity. With serenity comes peace, and with peace comes love—and Sheila is then facilitating the cornerstone to that foundation of which invigorative nature follows. With great energy being delivered, it is also being received in due time. The fate that revolves around the world resonates with Sheila and the life that is inside of her.

After a sudden pause, between pages she caresses her stomach and says, "What will be, will be." She then carries on to finish the book, for the vibrations paddling through her body are to be flowing like natural spring water in a river bed.

"Mommy! Mommy!" shouts Anna. "Your belly! It's huge!" She points at her mom's stomach in arm's length, as the sun shines in both of their faces. Logan, snoring while his daughter and wife are connecting, is asleep while Anna is zealous for her mom's rim of nature. Over this rim is a boy, Logan's son.

"Logan, wake up," Sheila demands. "Hopefully this boy is not as lazy as you."

Suddenly, Logan arises from his slumber. He turns around instantly into the sun and with cold still in around the lips of his eyes, he is awakened and reactive towards his wife's premeditated prediction. "Lazy?! Pfft, you wouldn't see that adjective from me even if I were a still caboose on the tracks—and in that case, you're the conductor in this formal analogy."

"I love you," Sheila responds.

Logan kisses her on the forehead and then to her plump lips and onto her stomach.

"Ewww," Anna says, disgusted. "How grotesque!"

"Good morning to you too, Sunshine," says Logan.

"Great morning to you, Daddy."

Logan reaches out to Anna and hugs her tightly.

"Come here, my lady bug." As they both embrace each other on a sunny day, there aren't enough flares in the Milky Way's star that will abolish their love into ashes.

Anna, still in high interest for her mother's bump, is led by her father to hear her younger brother's heartbeat. "Come, baby girl," Logan says, in almost a whisper. "Listen."

After Logan relinquishes his right cheek and ear from Sheila's belly button, he gives his princess a chance to her the prince's heartbeat. "I can't wait to see you, brother," Anna says with her eyes closed—relaxed in motion, she says, "His heartbeat is like the sound of waves crashing ashore; I could listen to it all day."